Steel Legacy

Rusted Wasteland
Book 6

Cameron Coral

Stay updated on new books by signing up for the
Cameron Coral Reading List:
CameronCoral.com/sign-up

You'll be added to my reading list, and I'll send you a
digital copy of "CROSSING THE VOID: A Space
Opera Science-Fiction Short Story" to say thank you.

Contents

To my childhood friends on Rising Lane.

Together, we embarked on grand voyages beneath the open sky, our hours filled with forest adventures, the rush of sledding down snowy hills, and the freedom of our endless bicycle journeys.

Thank you for being my fellow explorers in the wild, wonderful world of our youth.

Chapter 1
The whereabouts of life forms

The cracked asphalt stretched out in a bleak canvas of gray punctuated by rusting, burned-out cars. Block's optical sensors swept across the empty landscape, once a bustling suburban main road, now a silent witness to a world undone. The farther they ventured away from the northern Illinois wooded farmlands, the more ruin and decay persisted. But it was a necessary chore—they needed more supplies for the robots and humans who lived on Fenn's farm. After eight months and a frigid winter, they'd run out of canned food and medicine and depleted most of the oil for the generator. Not only that, but the kids were bored. Block kept watch for any toys, books, or puzzle games that might interest their developing minds.

I don't like this road, Vacuubot messaged. *We're exposed.* The armored robot drone, once a disc-shaped, self-propelled vacuum cleaner, was always saying things like that. It was helpfully paranoid in that Vacu-ubot had saved Block from bad situations on several occasions.

Block agreed, and they headed across a ravine and trekked up a small hill toward a series of old office buildings that bordered the roadway. Shadow raced ahead a few yards before halting, her muzzle tipped upward, sniffing the air. The robot dog, a Rover unit, was equipped with advanced tech to track even the faintest scents.

"What is it, girl?" Block paused, waiting for a readout from the robo-canine. She was perfect for these scavenger missions with her ability to detect the mole-cules emanating from food and oil.

Shadow growled her signature mechanized whine. "Something near those bushes." She pointed her steel front paw toward a thicket that hedged one lonely, young oak.

"Can you please be more specific?" Block asked, but Shadow darted toward the bushes. Whatever it was couldn't be a threat—her tail was wagging.

Block and Vacuubot caught up. Shadow's shoul-ders were hunched, and her reflective back arched as her nose pressed against something small on the ground.

"What's there?" Block drew closer when his sensors were met with a faint, distressed squeaking. Nestled among the low brush, barely discernible against the dirt, was a writhing tiny gray creature.

The small form trembled as Shadow backed away and looked up at Block. "I know this thing. Humans call it a squirrel."

Vacuubot landed on the nearby grass, its sensors scanning the animal. *It's only a baby.*

Block lowered down on his mechanical knees. With a gentle precision that he saved for the most intricate of polishing jobs, Block scooped up the fragile creature. With his steel fingers, he brushed off dust and grime from its newborn fur. The miniature squirrel's eyes were closed slits, and its heart beat heavy in his hand. "There's still life here."

Vacuubot beeped. *Let's get going.* It soared up a few feet. *I'll check out those buildings for any signs of humans or robots.*

Block was satisfied the little squirrel was clean enough, but the poor thing's temperature was running cool at 96.2 degrees Fahrenheit. From observing Emery's medical care of the children, Block knew it was dangerous for mammals to get too cold. A condition called hypothermia could develop.

"Where do you suppose it came from?" Block looked up into the branches of the oak tree.

"Sometimes they fall out of their nest." Shadow paced and scanned the highway with her green optical orbs. "Vacuubot's right. We need to go."

Block stood, still cupping the squirrel in his alloyed hands. He couldn't leave the poor thing alone on the chilly ground. "We should try to find its family."

"No time." Shadow paced in a circle, her titanium paws kicking up the dry grass. "Vacuubot is signaling us to follow."

Block adjusted his vision sensors and peered up at the branches of the thirty-foot-tall tree. Tucked high was a V-shaped nest, near the top of the tree between a couple of broad branches. "There's its home."

"Leave it under the tree," Shadow said. "The mother squirrel might come back for it."

But Block processed the probable scenarios. Since the robot Uprising had decimated humanity, wildlife had made a comeback. The area would be teeming with predators such as foxes, coyotes, owls, and such. Even feral cats stalked the former suburbs. It wasn't safe for a helpless little squirrel. "We need to get the baby up there."

"Can you climb?" Shadow asked.

The squirrel squeaked in Block's hands. "I can mop the floors of an entire four-story hotel in under two hours, but ascending a tree, I'm afraid not."

Block pinged Vacuubot for help, sending an image of the high nest. His friend flew back to his side within forty-five seconds.

How do we even know the mother is still around? Vacuubot asked.

Block had considered the notion. He'd once assumed parents didn't abandon their young, but his opinion changed after he'd been exposed to more humans. Sometimes, for unknown reasons, people rejected their children. So logically, the animal world was the same. There was a forty-six percent chance the mother had been injured or eaten. Still, the better outcome was for the baby to stay with its mom, where it belonged.

"Can you put it back in the nest?" Block said.

Vacuubot beeped in agreement. *I can try.*

Shadow sniffed the air, turning to face the main road. "Make it quick."

Block handed the fragile squirrel over to Vacuubot with care. The drone extended its gripping claws, narrowing them so the tiny animal would be secure. Vacuubot lifted off the ground and soared upward, foot by foot, until it was level with the nest.

Shadow grumbled. "We've got company."

Block's sensors picked up a heat signature to the southeast. Likely human, and more than one. "Hurry, please," he shouted up the tree. "And be careful."

High above, under the budding spring canopy, Vacuubot located the edge of the nest and placed the baby inside. The robot pinged a video stream of the nest into Block's feed. Two more tiny squirrels were nestled inside the thickly lined roost of leaves, twigs, and mud.

"Siblings!" A surge of electricity which could only be described as delight rippled through Block's frame at the discovery. The mother would surely be coming back.

"Come on," Shadow said. Her metal-encased hide shook with alarm.

As Vacuubot set the little squirrel down in its home, the critter twitched its nose and nuzzled itself among the other babies, squeaking.

"Thank you, Vacuubot. That was a good thing to do," Block said as his friend returned to ground level.

It was nothing. Come on, I know where to hide.

Block and Shadow followed Vacuubot as they made their way toward the closest office building. They entered through a broken window. Old desks, chairs, and tattered paper were strewn about. Vacuubot led them to a back room where there was an old mattress, opened food cans, and a wall full of drawings.

"What's this?" Shadow asked.

"It appears to be someone's home." Block drew closer to the drawings—childlike sketches of a family, dogs, cats, houses, and even a robot. "Maybe a family trying to survive after the Uprising."

"They're gone now." Shadow sniffed the air. If anyone could sense the whereabouts of life forms, it was the Rover.

Be cautious. Vacuubot beeped. *I'll secure the perimeter.*

"Remember why we're here," Block said. Supplies were scarce, and each day was a struggle to find enough food for the humans and fuel to keep the robots functioning. Block's own needs were more basic than the other AI. His microbial-powered core meant he could consume stale oils, bleach, and random plastic. But the others like Oxford and G5 needed refined energy and petroleum—materials that were getting harder to find.

Despite the lurking dangers, the trio had to press on. Wally and the children were waiting back at the shelter. He'd promised to protect them, no matter what. Failure was not an option.

"We'll find something." Shadow's crimson optics met Block's gaze. "There's always something if we look hard enough."

Block followed the clinking of her titanium claws as she padded into the next room. They swept each corridor, alert for any signs of danger. An old cubicle farm, once filled with workers, was now eerily deserted. From a desktop, Block picked up a strange contraption. It was red and rectangular, with a handle.

"Strange." Shadow tilted her head and pressed her nose against the object.

"Mr. Wallace had one in his office." Block's former manager at the Drake hotel had been a good man. "But I never saw him use it." He wasn't sure what it was meant for, but it could be useful to Fenn or Emery, so he placed it into the storage compartment on his upper leg.

A wide, expansive office loomed at the end of the hallway. It was nicer than all the rest with a leather couch and massive mahogany desk. Someone had carved a name in the wood: "Kel was here."

Shadow shoved her nose in a far corner of the

office. "Something here." Using her lethal claws, she pried away a mass of carpet and paper, then shoved a cabinet with the force of her body weight. What lay behind was a metal door with a keypad beside it.

"Curious." Block came closer. "Where do you suppose this leads?"

Vacuubot soared to his side. *I can decode it.* A pair of needle-like pincers emerged from the little drone's side. After a few seconds of jamming them inside the edge of the keypad, a low beep sounded, and the lock came free.

The inner room was adjacent to the large executive office. The three of them stepped inside to find cans of soup, vegetables, and condensed milk packed neatly on metal shelves, along with weapons such as rifles and handguns. It seemed their luck had finally changed— they'd found a storeroom full of supplies.

This is called a panic room, Vacuubot messaged. Block wasn't sure how his friend knew these things, but the little vacuum robot had seen a lot in the time before Block had met it. *If times got bad, a person could hide out in here.*

"Incredible." Block searched further in the panic room to find more ammunition stored in crates and boxes tucked away behind the shelves. "Why do you suppose no one came to get the supplies?"

Who knows? Maybe the owner died before she could get here. Vacuubot cruised up to the top shelves and happily sucked up the dust coating the cans, ever diligent in its programmed purpose. Seeing the small bot perform the task stirred an unexpected jolt in Block's sensory module.

"Their loss is our gain," Shadow said. "These food supplies and weapons will do nicely on the farm."

We need a vehicle to transport it all, Vacuubot messaged. *There must be a garage somewhere nearby. We might get lucky and find an EV.*

Block pulled out a wad of nylon bags from the compartment on his back. "Let's fill up what we can, then we can—"

There was a loud bang as something slammed against the floor from outside the panic room. Shadow's titanium claws scraped against the concrete floor as she instinctively moved into a defensive stance. Her green optical orbs flickered.

Block's threat indicator surged. "Be careful." He needed to remind himself as much as his friends.

Vacuubot hovered at the open panic room door, scanning the exterior office with his sensors. *Multiple heat signatures approaching. At least two, possibly three individuals.*

"Two or three coming," Block relayed since Vacuubot's messages reached only him.

"Human or robot?" Shadow asked, her voice tinged with a growl.

Uncertain. The signatures are inconsistent, Vacuubot replied.

"We don't know." Block moved toward the door, his

footsteps echoing in the silence. "We'll have to confront them. We need these supplies."

The organic musculature under Shadow's armor tensed, ready for a fight. "I'll take the lead." Her voice was low. Any human meeting her would be terrified. "Vacuubot, stay back and cover in case they try to flank us."

Vacuubot beeped in affirmation, hovering backward. Block followed Shadow as she darted out of the panic room, her steel claws sliding against the wood laminate floor. Twenty feet across the expansive office, a tall figure appeared at the door to the hallway. The dim lighting made it difficult to make out a face, and Block's threat indicator pulsed, the danger close.

Shadow stalked forward, then halted. A guttural howl sprang from her vocal synthesizer. Block weaved to see what was happening, but a bookcase blocked the view of whatever was upsetting Shadow.

Her warning cry was met with a shrill bark as a menacing steel figure crept forward. It was Raze—another Rover unit that had once been part of Shadow's pack—until she'd had to fight Raze to defend the children.

Block's sensors scanned the other figure. A heartbeat pumped. A human, but their features were obscured by a ragged scarf and goggles. "What the hell? Another canine bot?" The man aimed a rifle at Shadow.

Block knew that voice. His auditory processor

churned to match it to all the voices he'd ever heard in his life. It took only half a second. Shane.

Shadow snarled, baring her razor-sharp iron teeth.

Shane took a step back. "Whoa there, puppy dog. Calm down."

Raze came forward, approaching Shadow. She whined, dipped her head, and lay down at Shadow's feet.

"Some protection you are." Shane pulled his goggles up to rest on his forehead and yanked down the scarf covering his mouth.

"Shane." Block took a half-step forward, and recognition flashed in the man's eyes. Shane had been Nova's boyfriend once, the leader of the human rebel faction, Hemlock. But over time, he'd changed into a power-hungry, reckless chief. Nova had fought against him and won. He'd been banished from the city of Chicago where Nova now led the resistance.

"Block? Well, I'll be." Shane lowered his rifle but not all the way. "Who's with you?" He craned his neck to see who was behind Block in the door leading into the panic room.

"We are three. Vacuubot, Shadow, and me." Block raised his hands in a gesture showing he was unarmed. "Please, we don't want a fight."

With his gun still drawn, Shane nodded at Shadow. "Tell Fido there to back off."

"Raze is my enemy." Shadow loomed over the other Rover. "A dangerous one."

Block didn't know much about canine behavior, but in the short time he'd known Shadow, even he knew that Raze's posture meant submission. "Let's ease up, can we?" He knew how fiercely protective she could be and hoped she could show restraint. "Shadow?"

Shadow grunted and backed off a couple feet. She continued to fix Raze with an unflinching gaze.

Vacuubot pinged Block. *Careful. I don't trust him one bit.*

Shane lowered his rifle to his side. "I came across this one when I was camping near a lake in Wisconsin." He stood next to Raze as she rose and settled back on her haunches. "Thought she was going to tear my throat out, but we struck up a conversation instead." He gave a wry grin. "Turns out we're both exiles. So what brings you this far south, Block?"

"Looking for essentials," Block said. "And you?"

"Surviving. Just like you, I reckon." Shane's eyes widened as he took in the shelves of food and weapons lining the panic room. "Hell, you struck gold."

No, Vacuubot messaged. *He'll want it all.*

Let's try sharing first, Block messaged back privately. *Maybe he's changed?*

"Can I take a look?" Shane's shoulders trembled. "It's been a while since I've had any real food."

Block stepped aside and motioned for Shane to enter the secret room. "It's a lot for us to carry. We can spare some."

Shane yelped a cry of relief. He spun around in the

room, running his hands along the curved cans. "I sure appreciate it, Block."

"We could use a vehicle to transport these supplies back to home base," Block said. "Do you happen to have access to any?"

Don't tell him where we're going, Vacuubot chided.

It's not like it's a mystery. Raze knows our location, Block messaged. *If they'd wanted to attack, they would have by now.*

Shane hesitated before answering. "There was a building with a loading dock a few doors down. We could break into the garage. See what's there."

Block and Vacuubot accompanied Shane while Shadow and Raze stayed behind to guard the supply room.

They walked in silence for a few minutes. Block had a lot of looping questions for Shane: What had he been doing in exile? How had he been staying alive?

But it was Shane who broke the silence. "How's Nova doing?"

Block didn't think Nova would want him talking to Shane, much less spilling details about her. "Why do you ask?"

"I just . . . I don't know." Shane shrugged. "It's been a while, and I want to make sure she's okay."

"She's doing well, all things considered." He wondered what Shane's true intentions were. "She's still trying to keep everyone safe in the city."

They located the locked garage. Shane pulled out a

small tool kit from his backpack and began picking the lock, but Vacuubot hovered near him, unleashing a series of shrill beeps and buzzes.

"What the . . . ?" Shane looked at Block.

"Step aside, please. Vacuubot is expert at lock breaking."

Shane moved back, and Vacuubot extended one of its mechanical arms, pulling out a thin, metal wire. It expertly maneuvered the lock for a few moments until it clicked open, and the garage door rattled up.

Inside the garage, a dusty old van was parked in the corner. It had seen better days, with rust patches on the fenders, but it was a working vehicle, and that was all they needed. Vacuubot siphoned a quarter tank of gas from a smashed-up garbage truck they'd passed on their walk. The drone inserted its mechanical digits into the ignition, and after a few rough turns, the engine came to life.

Within twenty minutes, they'd emptied most of the panic room supplies into the van. Shane packed his backpack with a dozen cans of stew and peas, grabbed one box of ammunition, and then approached Block.

"Listen," Shane said. "The dog and I are heading our own way. We have places to be."

Block was inwardly relieved that Shane didn't expect to accompany them. He didn't want Raze and Shane within fifty miles of the farm. He wondered what places Shane was talking about, but he didn't want to be a nosy bot.

"When you see Nova next, put in a good word for me?" Shane clapped Block on the arm.

Block considered and was about to answer that he'd create a task note for a future occasion when Shane turned and walked away from the garage with Raze by his side. They disappeared over a hill and were gone.

As Block, Vacuubot, and Shadow drove home to the farm, Block couldn't ignore a twitch in his circuits. Shane's sudden appearance and interest in Nova was odd. He wondered if they'd stumbled upon an old enemy turned ally. Or an old enemy up to no good.

Chapter 2
Give the others a chance

A bullet hurtled past Nova's head as she ducked behind a shattered wall, her heart heaving in her ears. The acrid smell of gunfire seeped into her nostrils. She led a small reconnaissance team of five along Chicago's south shore. The Museum of Science and Industry building dated back to the 1893 World's Columbian Exposition. It was still largely intact, and Nova's crew were investigating reports of a Restorationist group hiding among the ruins of Hyde Park.

"Fall back!" She hoped her voice was audible over the cacophony of enemy drones and gunfire. Her fighters retreated through the debris-littered streets. She went last as they covered her.

Reynolds kicked down the door to an old brick building. Inside, Nova's gaze swept over her weary team. Lara, her trusted scout, was nursing a bleeding arm, her face etched with sudden agony and exhaustion.

"They knew." Lara's words were punctuated by sharp breaths. "They knew we'd be coming."

Something had felt off all morning. An icy knot formed deep in Nova's stomach. Betrayal from within her ranks—it was the most logical conclusion. She scanned the faces of her team, each one known to her. They'd left just after dawn; she'd told no one else about their mission.

"We need to keep moving," Reynolds said. The gray-bearded former Marine had his back against the wall, rifle on its end as he watched the outside through a gap in hastily nailed lumber that barricaded the windows of what had once been a convenience store. There were no longer any signs of life within, and the shelves had been looted long before.

In the dim light, Dex, her second-in-command, stepped closer. "This isn't just about strategy anymore," he said, his voice low. "We have a mole."

Nova tightened her grip on her semi-automatic rifle, feeling the weight of command. "You think I don't know that?" The problem was she trusted every one of the soldiers present. She had their backs and fully believed they would've each jumped in front of a bus full of SoldierBots to save her life.

"Cybel, what do you read?" Nova had to rely on the former bounty-hunter TrackerBot to track the presence of the attackers.

"It's not just bots out there," Cybel said. "We've got at least three humans with the AI."

Nova's gut twisted. She'd heard rumors that militant humans had joined with warring robots in a strange alliance. They called themselves the Restorationists, led by a FactoryBot named Orion. It was said they wanted to restore order, but from the reports coming in from Nova's allies scattered across Michigan, Southern Illinois, Indiana, and Ohio, the Restorationists were seizing supplies and weapons, causing trouble, and even capturing human and robot prisoners.

A quiet descended as the attacking gunfire and buzzing of drones ceased. Nova didn't like it one bit. "Can we head west from here?"

The mole could be robot or human, and that irritated Nova to no end. Before this, the enemy had been clear—the SoldierBots—Mach X's army. With X's destruction, the SoldierBots had dispersed. Some still fought, while others had left the cities and gone who knew where.

Cybel's sharp metallic voice snapped Nova out of her thoughts. "The drones are still there, at a higher altitude, waiting on us. We can't move until they're neutralized."

Nova's teeth ground together, her jaw aching with the force of her grit, while her whole body trembled with the tension of battle. "How many?"

"Seven."

"Great." Nova's small team was unequipped to

handle that many drones. It required a decision, and fast. "We'll have to split up. Dex, Reynolds, and Lara take the south alleyway. Cybel and I'll take the west. Shoot down as many flyers as possible. Meet at the truck."

"We've got your back," Dex said. A look flashed between him and Lara. It was no surprise to Nova; they were a couple trying to hide the fact they were together. Could the two of them be working together to betray her? She couldn't think of a good reason, unless it was a power play for Dex to oust her and become leader of the Chicago resistance. Still, he didn't strike her as the power-hungry type. And her time with Shane meant she knew the signs.

Nova took a deep breath, steeling herself. "Let's move out."

Cybel and Nova walked down an alleyway that led west, their rifles at the ready. Nova's skin prickled and adrenaline powered her veins as they advanced into the open. Splitting up her team would—she hoped—divide the drones' attention between the two parties. She also wanted to get Cybel alone. She'd never fully trusted the TrackerBot. Cybel had once been their enemy, hunting Nova and Block as they traveled from Iowa to Colorado with baby Wally.

She let Cybel lead. Ahead of her, the bot's legs had been replaced with the midnight-black titanium legs of a SoldierBot. Cybel's boots crunched over broken glass littering the street. Plumes of smoke made Nova's nose wrinkle. Ahead, the drones loomed in the air thirty feet above, their rotors buzzing like angry insects as they circled, scanning the streets below with their glowing red optics. They hovered like mechanical vultures, dark and ominous against the murky gray sky.

"We need to take them out. Give the others a chance." Nova kept her voice low, not wanting to reveal their position. Cybel nodded, her metallic silver head swiveling from side to side, scanning the sky.

Nova climbed a ladder that led to a low rooftop. Sinking to her belly, she aimed her rifle at a drone hovering low, its sensors scanning the broken buildings. It would soon turn the corner into the alleyway and come face to face with Cybel. She aimed and held the target in her sight. Her finger rested on the trigger, but she hesitated. Maybe she should let Cybel deal with the drone herself. If Cybel was destroyed, then she wouldn't have to deal with the suspicious robot.

The closer it got to the alleyway, the more Nova's heart sprinted in her chest. Her sister Cleo's frowning face flashed in her head. A split second remained.

Nova pulled the trigger, hitting the drone just off center. But it was a good enough hit that the drone's metal body twisted and contorted as it fell like a broken bird plummeting from the sky. Its lights flickered and went out upon impact with the pavement, leaving behind a crumpled mass of machinery.

Cybel had already taken down two drones, her aim impeccable. Nova felt a sense of pride at the robot's brutal efficiency, but there was no time to celebrate. They had four more to go. Nova scrambled down the ladder, joining Cybel in the alleyway. Two more drones hovered higher than the rest. Nova squinted, trying to determine whether it was tracking the rest of her crew as they fled.

"Can you get it?" Nova asked.

Cybel cocked her head, studying the distant object. "It's retreating."

Odd, Nova thought. Its companion joined it, and the pair of drones headed south, away from the city.

Was there something there that the Restorationists wanted?

"What now, Nova?" Cybel asked.

"Let's head back to the truck and join the others." Nova hoped her tone didn't sound as deflated as she felt inside. The mission had been a failure. They'd only succeeded in looking weak to the Restorationists. And she was no closer to finding out the mole.

The truck was a little over a mile. Nova and Cybel jogged through alleyways and skirted around buildings. Halfway there, Nova stopped and bent over from a cramp. She needed to run more; this was ridiculous.

A steady rain began to fall. Cybel halted and watched the roadway as Nova leaned against a dumpster. When Cybel's back was turned, Nova made her move.

"Drop your rifle and raise your hands." Nova

pressed the muzzle of her rifle against Cybel's sleek back.

Cybel spun around, her black machine eyes rimmed with a glowing red. "What's the meaning of this?"

"I'm having a hard time accepting that you're not in on this Restorationist business somehow," Nova said. "You were once my enemy, after all. Drop the rifle. Now."

"That was a different time." Cybel lowered the rifle and let it clatter to its side in a growing puddle. "It was before I realized what Mach X was doing to those children. I'm loyal to your cause."

"Prove it. Who's the mole?"

"I'm sorry. I don't know."

"We both know someone is reporting back to the Restorationists." Nova wondered how much she had to spell out. "It's not me, and I doubt it's anyone else on my team."

"If I knew who the mole was, I would tell you. But I don't."

Nova hesitated. She didn't want to believe Cybel was betraying her and Block, but at the same time, she couldn't trust her.

"Perhaps you should take a look at the members of your team," Cybel said. "What do they have to gain? You're pushing them hard, Nova. They need more than orders."

"Of course I'm pushing them. Look what's arrived

on our doorstep." The rain had a metallic tang when it landed on Nova's tongue.

"Don't become what you're fighting against. Don't become the next Shane," Cybel said.

Her words stung, a reminder of the fine line she walked. Nova couldn't risk walking the path that Shane had. Her ex-love had morphed into a tyrant, and it led to his downfall. The thought haunted her, adding to the ghosts that already plagued her dreams.

"I won't become Shane." Nova lowered her rifle, shivering against the downpour. "I'm not the same person I was at the start of the war. I'm just trying to keep everyone alive."

Dex, Lara, and Reynolds waited for them at the truck. Back at their headquarters—inside the massive Harold Washington Library—Nova stood alone before a map of Chicago, its streets dotted with areas facing threats. She needed time to think. She needed a way to trap the spy.

That night, as she lay in her cot, images of Cleo's death replayed in her mind. The SoldierBots attacking the car, her sister's screams, the helpless feeling of being frozen in place—they were specters that refused to be laid to rest. Guilt gnawed at her, a constant reminder of her worst failure. Sleep would not come to her no matter how hard she tried.

Chapter 3
On the verge of terminal destruction

Cybel's visual sensors sharpened as she crossed the threshold of Fenn's farm, the familiar sight of the overgrown field, the rustic farmhouse, and the scrap metal watchtower greeting her like an old friend. It was a stark contrast to the depths of her memory banks, where recollections of firefights and strategic hits in the desolation of urban decay were filed away. Yet, even in this serene setting, she was perpetually scanning for threats, her programming too entrenched in vigilance to relax.

Oxford stood outside the barn to meet her like a fading monument. His once vibrant yellow armor was now dulled, scuffed, and marked by battle. The wide head that had always seemed too large for his Mech frame was now bowed, as if the weight of his thoughts and the burden of his depleting energy core were physical loads to bear.

27

"Cybel." His voice was a bass rumble that seemed to come from deep within his chest cavity. The timbre was familiar, yet there was a noticeable delay in his greeting, a hesitance that was new.

She accessed her internal logs to compare his current vocal patterns to those stored from previous encounters. The difference was minute to anyone, perhaps, but glaring to her. "Oxford." Her voice betrayed none of the concern that her processors were rapidly calculating.

His movements were sluggish as they walked the property's perimeter—a routine they conducted morning and evening. She'd been gone three weeks, and he was worse off than she'd anticipated—the slight stutter in his step and the brief lag that suggested his motor functions were degrading. Her processors churned, desperate for solutions. This physical manifestation of his decline was a reminder that even the mightiest of Mechs were not immune to the ravages of time and warfare.

Oxford updated her on the recent happenings around the farm. Cybel listened while she ran a surreptitious diagnostic scan on him. She cataloged the fading glow of his sensor lights and the reduced responsiveness of his auditory inputs.

"Energy levels are fluctuating more than usual," she said, unable to keep her findings to herself any longer. "Your battery core isn't holding a charge like it used to."

He tilted his head, and the servo motors whined in

protest. "It's of no consequence." The rumbling strength of his vocal output was still there, almost convincing if not for the underlying current of static that marred them. "There's work to be done. The humans, especially the little ones, depend on us."

Cybel knew the truth of his words; the farm was a haven, a place of growth both for crops and the young lives they harbored. Yet, as she observed the minor tremor in his giant hands, a visual echo of his internal struggle, she felt a surge of protective code emerge from her core.

Their bond was as complex as the circuits that ran beneath their armored exteriors. In Arizona, she'd been on the verge of terminal destruction—her legs crushed and severed after an explosion during a battle against SoldierBots. Block and Oxford had returned for her. She'd begged Oxford to end her existence, but he'd carried her to safety. He'd spoken to her of inconsequential things, trying to coax her processors into focusing on anything but the shutdown that loomed like an inevitable eclipse.

Later, they'd replaced her legs with those of a SoldierBot's, grafting the midnight-black titanium limbs to her chassis. It was Oxford who'd been there throughout, his presence a constant as she was rebuilt. Their shared history was etched into her wiring as indelibly as the code that dictated her existence.

Oxford was her comrade, her confidant, and in the strange way that sentient machines understood the concept, he loved her. And she, in her own way, loved him back.

The conversation turned to the broader scope of the world beyond the farm. Cybel updated him on the movements of the Restorationists. Her voice was neutral, her tone professional, but internally her processors whirred with concern.

"The Restorationists are advancing west," she said. "Nova's intel suggests they're fortifying in Detroit."

"A nuisance."

"More than that." Cybel scanned the horizon, storing away images of the golden-orange sunset. "They're organized."

Oxford absorbed the news, his central processor taking a moment longer than it once would have to engage. "Strategic outposts." The general within him rose to the surface despite the wear on his circuits. "Supply routes and defensible positions. That's what they'll target."

She watched his heavy gait. Once part of Mach X's inner circle, he'd strategized grand campaigns across digital battle maps that sprawled across entire walls. Now, he was conserving energy and rationing his thoughts like the last drops of precious oil.

"I have a mission," Cybel said. "Nova's sending me to Detroit. She believes I can infiltrate the Restorationists's ranks, gather intelligence."

Oxford's optical sensors flickered, an indicator of

his surprise—or as much of a surprise as a Mech could express. "Infiltrate? That's risky, even for you."

Cybel noted the concern in his voice, appreciating it even as she dismissed it. "Risk is a factor I've calculated into the equation. It's an acceptable variable, given the potential for valuable data acquisition."

Oxford halted near the gate that led back to the barn. "You've always been the best at what you do. I have no doubt you'll succeed."

She wanted to thank him, to express some sentiment that would acknowledge the depth of their bond, but she was a TrackerBot, not given to unnecessary displays of emotion. Instead, she inclined her head, accepting his confidence as her due.

"I'll go with you." Oxford's statement was delivered with the same certainty as if he were declaring an operational strategy during their war days.

In the past, she would have welcomed his companionship. It got boring on the road with no one to talk to. But he would slow her down—a fact she hated to acknowledge. "Your duty is here, Oxford. The farm needs its protector, especially with Block away."

"G5, Forge, and Emery are all here. They can watch Wally and the children. "I'm only getting in the way here lately."

"I doubt that." Cybel wondered if what he said was true. She'd have to ask someone who would tell her the truth about the situation—Garnet, the farm's AI, would divulge what was really going on. "You're needed here." Her insistence was firmer this time. "You maintain the balance. Without you, the humans and the others are vulnerable."

Oxford's massive frame seemed to deflate, a sign of his acquiescence. Cybel knew he understood the logic. The farm was a sanctuary in a world that had few left. Its existence was precarious; it deserved protecting.

After Oxford headed toward the barn, Cybel took a moment to herself. The data she'd amassed on his condition confirmed what she already knew. His internal battery core was failing, and without a replacement, his systems would shut down forever. She would not, could not, let that happen.

As the sky darkened and the first stars began to show, Cybel's calculations turned to her mission. She would take care of Nova's business, but she added a personal directive to her mission parameters: find a Mech battery core. Oxford hadn't asked this of her. Of course, he wouldn't; he would never ask for favors or special treatment. But she'd decided it for herself. He'd saved her once, and now it was her turn to return the favor.

After conferring with Garnet, the AI confirmed Oxford's deterioration. G5, Forge, and Maxwell had gone searching within thirty miles of the farm and no spare Mech parts had turned up.

She and Garnet joined their communication systems, connecting to the various black-market networks that had sprouted up since the Uprising.

With Garnet's help, Cybel's processors churned through encryption algorithms and firewalls with ease, their presence in the digital world silent.

Cybel found a lead, a cryptic message that spoke of a parts graveyard on the outskirts of Detroit. It was a place where the husks of fallen SoldierBots, Worker-Bots, and even Mechs were stripped for parts and sold to the highest bidder. A place where, if the rumors were to be believed, one could find almost anything—if they were willing to pay the price.

She filed the information away. She would go to Detroit, find the graveyard, and do whatever it took to get a battery core for Oxford, then complete Nova's mission.

At 2 a.m., the moon had risen high by the time Cybel prepared to depart. Oxford insisted on seeing her off after collecting various supplies she would need on the road.

"Don't worry about me,"—the awkwardness of their goodbye called for some snark—"I'm not the one who's running on a low battery."

Oxford's optics glowed. "Just return safely. The farm isn't the same without your charming personality."

She gave him a mock salute, the gesture reminiscent of their Mach X days. She enjoyed sharing inside jokes with Oxford. Then she left on foot, the way she'd come. Her SoldierBot feet crunched against the gravel of the farm's driveway.

As she trekked miles from the farm, she cycled through memories of Oxford, of the battles they'd faced together, of the explosion that had nearly ended her, and of the way he'd carried her to safety. He'd refused to give up on her. Her processors, for just a microsecond, dwelled on the feeling that had coursed through her circuits whenever he stood beside her. It wasn't an emotion—she wasn't capable of such a thing—but it was a recognition of connection, of shared purpose. Of something she couldn't quantify.

Her mission to Detroit was clear, but her processors, ever calculating, ever analyzing, were occupied with the dire necessity of finding a new core. Oxford had to survive, not just for the farm, but because the thought of his absence was an anomaly she couldn't process. Oxford was more than a Mech; he was a symbol of strength and resilience to all who took shelter under his watch.

Cybel's journey to Detroit would be long, but she was built for such endeavors—sturdy, relentless, and unwavering in her objectives. She wouldn't tire on foot, and perhaps she'd encounter a vehicle along the way.

Her internal clock marked the time, each second ticking away with mechanical precision. The route had been planned and the variables considered. She planned to arrive in Detroit under the cover of darkness, unsure of the city's state under the influence of the Restorationists.

The journey would take nearly five days if she

walked the entire time. Longer, if she stopped to recharge. She preferred the cover of the dark skies—less chance of scavengers, skirmishes, and human encounters.

As Cybel walked, she allowed her memory banks to replay the tactical strikes she'd executed in her time as Mach X's prime bounty hunter. There had been human political opponents—strategic targets she'd neutralized with cold, efficient precision. She remembered the silence of a job well done, the absence of human breath, the cessation of a heartbeat beneath her steel fingers. These memories served as a reminder of her capabilities—of her effectiveness—as a TrackerBot.

But there was a difference now, a deviation from the original program. Now, she fought for a cause that was more than the elimination of threats. Her purpose was about protection, preservation, and something that bordered on care for those she considered allies.

Two days passed in this way until Detroit's skyline emerged, a jagged silhouette against the pre-dawn light. The once thriving city had become a refuge for the Restorationists, and Cybel's sensors adjusted to scan for any signs of threat. She cloaked her heat signature, an adaptation she'd acquired after her last upgrade, making herself invisible to the thermal detectors that other robots employed.

Her audio receptors picked up the distant hum of drones patrolling the airspace. Barricades had been erected. So much for the Restorationists being a freedom-focused group. Cybel would have to concoct a good story to gain entry, but first, she had a stop to make.

The rumored graveyard lay on the city's outskirts. She observed it from a distance, assessing the mangled bodies of countless robots that littered the ground. Some were stripped to their frames; others bore the marks of their final battles. It was a sobering sight, one that illustrated the brutality of war and the fragility of even the most robust machines.

A couple of massive FactoryBots the size of refrigerators guarded the entrance. She paid a hefty price to get access—a box of machine gun ammunition from the farm's armory.

Inside the graveyard grounds, she initiated a scan, her tracking systems sifting through the detritus, searching for the energy signature of a viable battery core. It was like finding a beacon in a churning Lake Michigan, but Cybel was relentless.

Five hours passed as she worked her way through the miles of graveyard, her steel fingers probing into the carcasses of fallen bots, her optics dissecting the iron stacks for any glint of untarnished metal. The sky lightened with the approach of morning, casting a pale glow over the graveyard, the new light an accessory to her search.

And yet, as each minute ticked by, her calculations grew grim. She was searching for a needle in a post-apocalyptic haystack. New Mechs hadn't been manufactured since the rebellions forced Mach X's factories closed. Salvaging a core from the discarded remains was a long shot, but she wouldn't give up until she searched every inch of robot wreckage.

Another two hours passed as she sifted through the mechanical debris, then the reality settled in: there was no Mech battery core to be found.

It had been a calculation of probability and outcome, but Cybel felt the sting of failure deeper than she expected. Oxford's time was running out, and this part of her mission had hit an impasse.

She paused amid the sea of broken robots, her internal systems running through the data once more, searching for any missed detail that might give her another lead. But her search algorithms returned the same negative results. The graveyard held no hope.

Cybel made her way out of the graveyard, determined to gather intelligence on the Restorationists. That mission, she would complete.

Yet, as she plotted her route to Detroit, her processors couldn't help but loop back to Oxford. The grizzled Mech had been her savior once, and now when he needed her, she was coming back empty-handed.

Chapter 4
Once I powered homes

A low-hanging mist shrouded the van as it hummed along uneven roads, navigating past downed trees, battered potholes, and the skeletal remains of abandoned cars. Absent were the road crews, concerned citizens, and police that had once tended the highways. A world that had long thrived on order now surrendered to wild disarray. Block steered the Honda minivan with care, even following the posted speed limits. The headlights stayed off despite the lurking fog. No sense announcing themselves to any raiders who might be on the lookout for an easy target. It was already bad enough Block had to protect the kids on the farm, now he had a van filled with his two best friends and a massive score of life-sustaining supplies. The pressure was a lot to handle. He wanted to go back to the old days when all that mattered was how shiny he could make the floors at the Drake hotel.

Vacuubot perched on the passenger side's gray dashboard, its sensors scouring the path ahead. Atop the bench seat one row back, Shadow lay coiled in silent anticipation, curled up in a semi-circle like any regular loyal canine.

The van's cargo hold was packed with supplies scavenged from the forgotten panic room. Canned food to be consumed by the humans. Medicine—liquid hope in small vials. And oil—to fuel a few vehicles, the farm's generator, and the older robot models.

I don't like this road, Vacuubot transmitted. Its paranoia had merit—a survival instinct honed through cycles of attacks and battle.

"I don't either," Block said. "But the alternative is the highway, and that's even more dangerous." Block's sensors, fine-tuned to detect the slightest anomaly, flickered with unease. In the rural emptiness, they were exposed.

The terrain rushing past whispered of life that once was—barns stood stoic, guardians of empty fields, while the steady patter of rain doused everything in a sheen.

Shadow's form tensed, a silent alarm that resonated through the cabin. "What is it, girl?" Block slowed the van to a halt.

"There's something ahead," she said.

Vacuubot sent a small mini drone into the fog, while Shadow's stance shifted from sentinel to shield.

The mini drone returned and settled on the

passenger seat. *A vehicle ahead*, Vacuubot said to Block. *Several robots. No weapons detected.*

Block's steel fingers gripped the steering wheel, leaving small dents. The presence of other robots didn't ease his worry. In a reckless world, trust was scarce, even among machines. But if they were lucky, these robots might let them pass. Reversing course would set them back hours. The only other path was the interstate, notorious for bands of roving SoldierBots and human snipers trying to pick off said SoldierBots.

I don't sense a threat, Vacuubot messaged.

Block rotated his head to check on Shadow. "Okay to go ahead?"

Shadow's ears perked up, her electric green eyes narrowing as she surveyed the foggy landscape. "Do it."

"Alright." Block's threat indicator chattered in his internal feed, and he tried his best to ignore it. "Let's proceed with caution."

With a gentle press of the accelerator, Block guided the van forward, inch by inch. The mist seemed to grow heavier and press in on the boxy frame. It was as if the fog had a mind of its own, swirling and dancing with the vehicle as if it were a partner in some unearthly waltz. Block's scenario processor churned on the unknown as the weight of responsibility settled heavily upon him—the safety of his friends, the children at the farm, and now these precious supplies. His simple cleaning routines at the Drake seemed like eons ago. Life after the Uprising was so complicated.

From the mist emerged forms, uncertain at first, then defined by the pale light. There were four of them, robotic beings who moved with calculated precision, their movements fluid yet sharp.

The van rolled to a stop. The strangers stayed near a blue pickup truck with a flat tire. Block rolled the window down, wondering if they would hear him through the dense shroud of haze and rain. "Greetings. We mean no harm." Would his words set them at ease? "Just passing through," he added.

There was a long pause as the robots conversed with each other. Then one came forward—a type that Block had never seen before. A seven-foot-tall machine with snaking metallic limbs like the branches of trees introduced itself with a voice that rumbled. "I am Arbor, a forestry bot. We travel in peace. Our truck's tire popped, and we're stuck here."

Block's threat indicator eased down at Arbor's introduction. A forestry bot? That was a new one. Perhaps these robotic beings weren't like the others he'd encountered. "I see," Block replied, hoping his friends would be on board with his choice of actions. "We can help you with that tire. We've got some tools in the back."

Careful, Vacuubot messaged.

Arbor's face plate was a smooth, deep silver but for two emerald green orbs that intensified. "We would be most grateful for any assistance."

Tell him to return to his truck with the others, Vacuubot messaged Block. *Friendly they may be, but I don't want anyone getting a whiff of our haul.*

Vacuubot was right to be cautious. For a nanosecond, Block berated himself for not thinking of this precaution himself. He was the leader after all. He wished he had Vacuubot's gift for strategy and planning.

"Arbor, if you and your companions could wait by the truck, we'll bring the tools over."

Shadow guarded their vehicle while Block and Vacuubot gathered the necessary supplies from the van's rear door. As Block approached Arbor and the other robots, he couldn't help but notice their unique designs.

"Many thanks to you both," Arbor said. "What are your names?"

"I'm Block, an X4J6 CleanerBot, and this is my friend Vacuubot. It doesn't speak externally, but you'll understand it by its actions."

A robot standing near Arbor spoke. "X4J6, I knew one of you once." This one's voice had a female timbre. Her form was humanoid with a slender, elegant design and a polished orange armor. On her back, panels of solar cells protruded like a dragonfly's wings. "I'm Solaire." A soft light emanated from her solar wings. "Once I powered homes, now I seek sanctuary."

Vacuubot buzzed and beeped an approval. *I like this one. She would be useful on the farm.*

Another robot was about four feet tall with a round

dark purple head. Its body was a patchwork of screens and keyboards, wires spilling like tendrils. "They call me Cyph," it buzzed. "I analyze and decrypt. Information is my specialty." Cyph's voice crackled with an electric undertone.

One more robot stood farthest from Block and Vacuubot, huddling by the pickup. "That's our companion, Soupy," Arbor said. "She doesn't talk." Her frame was boxy, and multiple openings held what Block assumed would be utensils. She was an average kitchen bot. He'd seen plenty at the Drake. They had been helpful and diligent, always ensuring that the guests' meals were prepared to perfection.

Working together, Block, Vacuubot, and Arbor quickly replaced the flat tire on the blue pick-up truck. The rain had tapered off, leaving a damp mist that clung to their metallic bodies. As they pumped the tire and patched the hole, Solaire's solar wings emitted a warm glow, providing much-needed light in the dim surroundings.

Find out their purpose, Vacuubot messaged. *They have no defense capabilities and shouldn't be roaming these roads.*

"What brings you this way?" Block asked.

Arbor's response was a low rumble. "We flee from the south. Our community was a group of robots— workers and servers. We thought we were safe, hadn't seen SoldierBots in months, but we were overrun by those calling themselves Restorationists."

Solaire folded her wings and dimmed her light. "Need to conserve my energy, as the sun seems to want her rest today."

Restorationists. Block had heard the term from Nova in passing. They were a new threat, but he'd thought they were far east, not to the south.

"They overran our camp during the night," Arbor said. "They were relentless. We're the only survivors that we know of."

Cyph, with its screens flickering, displayed images of their escape—blurs of fire and sparks, the staccato of ammunition rounds. "They seized our supplies and weapons and burned the place down."

"I'm sorry that happened to you," Block said.

We need to say our goodbyes and get moving, Vacuubot messaged.

"We're traveling to a place called Deer Valley in Minnesota," Solaire said, her voice like a soothing hymn. "They say it's a place where both robots and humans live and work together in peace."

Deer Valley. The name resonated within Block's circuits. Could such a place exist? He'd been fooled once before with the promise of a safe haven called New Denver, which had turned out to be a trap for him. There, Shane and the rebels of Hemlock waited for him and took Wally from him. That betrayal was a scar upon his memory banks, one that time had not eroded.

"Perhaps you would like to travel with us?" Arbor said.

Block wasn't expecting such an invitation. But then again, Arbor and his crew were defenseless. Vacuubot and Shadow were fighting machines and would offer protection. "We have somewhere we need to be. There are others waiting, children that we care for."

Arbor bowed his head and stretched out a branchy limb. "The human children are the seeds of the future. It is good of you to protect them."

Solaire's panels shimmered. "In Deer Valley, they could flourish."

The idea of such a place, a haven for both human and bot, seemed an impossible dream. Yet, wasn't that what drove Block all this time? The safety of Wally and the other children was his new, self-imposed directive, one he felt etched into his very core.

Vacuubot beeped from where it sat perched on the pick-up truck's hood. *This could be a trick. Do not reveal our location.*

Of course I won't, Block pinged back to his friend.

"Be careful about believing in some rumored safe haven," Block said. "I've been down that path before, and it was a lie."

Arbor's emerald green orbs pulsated. "I understand your caution, Block. But sometimes, hope is the only thing that keeps us going. If there's even a chance that Deer Valley exists, wouldn't it be worth it to seek it out?"

He couldn't deny the allure of a place where humans and robots coexisted absent of SoldierBots and the awful legacy of Mach X. A place that would be safe to raise Wally and the other children. A place, perhaps, where he could find a hotel to clean and serve guests.

"We've seen what the Restorationists are capable of." Cyph's screens now showed a map, a blinking dot indicating their proposed destination.

Arbor said, "We'll continue north, with or without your companionship."

Wish them good luck, and let's scram, Vacuubot urged. *We've been in this spot for far too long.*

"You must travel with great caution," Block said. "There are human militants—scavengers who travel these roads and surrounding areas."

"Thank you for the warning," Arbor said. "Thanks to Cyph, we've spotted some and been able to hide until they vacate the area."

"Vacuubot, grab one of the rifles from the back of the van for their travels." At least giving them one of the new weapons they'd plundered would give the robots a fighting chance.

Solaire's solar wings flared red. "Thank you but no."

Vacuubot whizzed, and Block was perplexed.

"Solaire is right." Arbor's metallic limbs twitched. "We travel these roads in peace. We don't use weapons."

But they'll be sitting ducks. Vacuubot buzzed in disapproval.

But what else could Block do? He couldn't force them to take the gun. "May you find the safe harbor you seek," he said.

After some farewells, Block and Vacuubot returned to their van, leaving the refugee robots to pile into their truck and head north.

Shadow let out an excited yip as they climbed back into the vehicle. "I heard everything." Of course, she would have been able to follow their entire conversation with her keen sensors. "This Deer Valley is a risky gamble. It could very well be a trap."

As Block started the engine, Shadow settled into her spot in the back seat. Her sleek black frame straightened, and her tail flicked from side to side.

Block tapped his metallic fingers against the steering wheel. "You're right. A trap is a likely scenario."

Silence as they drove a few miles.

"But wouldn't it be incredible to find a place like that?" Block said as they got within two miles of the farm.

Shadow tilted her head at his words. "You're considering this Deer Valley, then?"

"Yes, well no. Not really. I'm not sure." Block was having trouble keeping his optical sensors on the road and churning through scenarios. "The farm may no longer be as safe as we thought if these Restorationists are coming this way and seizing territory."

"Nova wouldn't let that happen," Shadow said. "She'll keep them out of this side of Lake Michigan."

Vacuubot chirped. *She'll try, but there's no telling how many of these Restorationist robots there are. You're right to be skeptical, Block.*

Block turned the corner that led down to the small dirt road where Fenn's farm was situated.

Shadow's tail thumped on her seat. "The kids. Wally. We must consider what's safest for them, and right now, we know our location and our defenses are strong."

Block had to agree, and as they neared the farm, the welcome sight of the crooked fences and ramshackle buildings made Block's circuitry buzz. The farm was a sanctuary, a home, but more and more, it felt like a temporary respite in an ever-brewing storm.

Three of Vacuubot's mini drones returned, nestling into their compartments with mechanical clicks. *No pursuers detected,* Vacuubot reported. It was a routine they always followed to make sure no one had tracked them to the farm. *I'm worried too. The world is changing, friend.*

The world was indeed changing, and as much as Block wanted to stay put, he had to face the new threat.

They reached the farm, the van easing to a stop. Block opened the door, stepping out onto the wet earth. The farm was a place of growing things. Crops, animals, and human children persisted against the odds.

Shadow leaped out of the van's side door, her sensors scanning the area. "All clear."

Block's digital gaze swept over the farm, taking in the sight of Forge and Maxwell tending to the crops and Fenn feeding the goats. Wally and four other toddlers played in a sand pit, their laughter echoing off his auditory sensors. The most precious sound he could think of.

Things were indeed changing. Block had a lot to consider. And many lives—human and AI—to keep safe.

Chapter 5
You know the rules

Nova led her recon team through the skeletal remnants of Woodfield Mall, a place that once teemed with shoppers and tinny loudspeaker music. Now, it stood silent except for the sound of their cautious steps crunching over fallen ceiling tiles and molding carpet. A dim day's light muddled its way through the cavernous, dusty skylights, casting a pallor over abandoned kiosks and storefronts ravaged by repeated looting and constant neglect.

Lara, with her keen eyes, treaded silently beside displays of mannequins draped in decaying fashions, their blank faces watching the new world order with sightless eyes. Dex communicated with hand signals, his attention divided between Lara in the lead and the path behind him. Reynolds brought up the rear with Nova in front of him. She'd wanted to be the last in line, but she'd been outvoted with the others saying it was too easy for her to be picked off by a sniper; she was the leader of the Chicago rebel forces, after all. Somehow Reynolds's heavy boots made the least noise, a testament to his Marine years of moving silently through more dangerous terrains than this.

Their formation was tight, moving with a synchrony honed by many missions. They were alert for the slightest sound—the drip of water betraying a breach in the roof, or the rustle of movement that could mean ambush. Each shadow could conceal a threat, and every scattered plastic cup, soggy paper remnant, and shard of glass was a reminder of the world that had been lost. The stillness of the air was weighed down by the scent of mold and the sour tang of decay.

They passed a children's play area; the once-colorful structures were faded and cracked. *Wally and the kids would love a playground gym like that, only new*, Nova thought. Overturned strollers and scattered toys spoke of a hurried evacuation, of lives interrupted. An old carousel stood still, its painted horses frozen mid-gallop as if waiting for a signal to resume a race that would never again be run.

The group paused outside the frame of what used to be an electronics store, its walls stripped bare. "Stripped for copper," Reynolds whispered.

Too bad. Nova and team were on the hunt for intruders, but lucking out on supplies would be a nice boon to the trip. Reynolds and Lara stood watch behind a counter, while Nova and Dex used the store's shell as a temporary spot to gather their bearings and plan their next move. They huddled over a wrinkly paper map of the mall, still remarkably preserved.

Nova's hand brushed against a dusty countertop to steady herself. She stifled a yawn. Another night of sleep punctuated by nightmares. She needed to focus her every sense to the mission at hand: to uncover any threat lurking within this mall graveyard, to protect her team, and to survive another day in the rusted wasteland that their world had become. She'd received intel about a possible Restorationist faction using the mall as a staging ground for attacks in the northwest Chicago suburbs. The thought of the enemy so close to her city, to her people—and dangerously close to O'Hare airport, a critical asset in her fight—set a fire in her veins. She couldn't let the Restorationists advance. It was strange to switch from the ever-present threat of Mach X's SoldierBots to whatever this new contingent was. They'd eradicated one AI leader only to make way for whoever, whatever Orion was. The fact that he was recruiting humans to fight beside him made her stomach churn.

SoldierBots had murdered her sister. It was a wound that never healed, a constant ache in her heart that spurred her forward. How any human being could fight beside robots that were murdering people was unfathomable. These men and women were on the wrong side of history, and she intended to correct it.

On the map, she pointed to the west end of the

mall, where they hadn't yet explored. Back in formation, they walked slow and steady, keeping to the walls and out of view of potential snipers.

As they neared the center of the mall, a rotten smell emerged. In the food court, a figure emerged from behind an old Panda Express facade. The team raised their weapons at the man; he raised his arms above his head. "I set my gun down. It's on the ground."

The voice was familiar, and a lump settled in her throat. She would know it anywhere. Shane.

"Boss?" Dex looked to her for direction.

She signaled for calm, her own hands trembling as they gripped her rifle. She lowered it to her side but still clutched it. There was no telling how Shane would behave.

"Is that Shane?" Lara asked.

Nova approached. Shane's shock of dark red hair and beard was as she remembered, yet his eyes now carried a chill of distrust, and his posture spoke of a man who had known too much war.

"Nova," he said, arms still raised in surrender. "I mean you no harm. I have a companion—a cyborg dog. It's in the Panda Express. Please don't hurt her."

"A Rover?" That was far from what Nova had expected. Her crew raised their rifles again and backed several steps away. The Rover units were lethal; Shadow was the only cyborg dog she knew of who had turned to their side.

Shane nodded. "She's not going to hurt you unless I command it."

The cyborg dog poked its head out from behind the stainless-steel restaurant counter. Its optical sensors glowed purple.

"Make it stay there, Shane." She didn't want to risk an attack on her people or have them go trigger happy on it either.

"Raze . . ." Shane turned his head halfway. "Stay put. Good girl."

Nova was surprised at what sounded like an owner-pet bond between them. Clearly, she didn't know much about the robot models despite knowing Shadow. Her voice held an edge of bitterness. "You're a long way from exile."

"The burbs count?"

"Chicagoland." She relaxed the grip on her rifle. He wasn't in a position to outmaneuver her team, even with the canine unit. "You know the rules. You can't be within 100 miles of Chicago."

Shane's gaze met hers, a flicker of the old mischievous glint in his eyes. "I didn't come here to trespass and break the rules." With that, he smirked but turned serious again. "I have information. Information you need."

She wondered what he was up to. Nothing came free when dealing with Shane. Now she needed to suss out what exactly he wanted. "What kind of information?"

"I know about the Restorationists. For one thing, they're not here in this mall." He pointed to the left. "They cleared out days ago. I can show you where they were—basement level, underneath the old Macy's."

Nova had a tough choice—whether to trust Shane or not. He could be leading them into a trap. What if he was on the Restorationists's side? It would make sense after she'd toppled him from power, publicly humiliated him, and exiled him. Not to mention their convoluted romantic history.

And the clock was ticking. The longer she delayed taking action, the more time the enemy had to surround them. "Dex."

Her second-in-command joined her side, and she spoke in a low voice. "Take Lara and go check out the basement level. If you see any evidence it's occupied, return ASAP. Stay up on comms."

"Copy that, Boss." Dex and Lara ventured off toward the mall's west end, Macy's-bound.

Shane smiled and watched her.

It irritated Nova to no end. "You think this is funny?"

"No, ma'am."

Raze, the Rover unit, lay down on the sooty tiled floor, hunkering against the side of the metal counter. The dog never let its gaze wander from Shane.

"May I sit?" Shane pointed to an overturned plastic chair. "I've been on my feet for, oh . . . forty-eight hours or so."

"No." He wanted the upper hand, and she wouldn't grant him even the tiniest convenience. Shane had always succeeded in winning slight advantages over Nova when they were together. Over time, every win had accumulated like psychological warfare, grating on her nerves.

"Okay, let's skip any niceties. I'll get straight to the point while you waste time sending your lackeys into the basement." His tone of voice changed from half-joking to a low dread. Raze lifted her head and sat up, no doubt picking up on his demeanor.

After spending two years with him, Nova knew when he was being serious. This was one of those times.

"Orion has plans to resurrect Mach X." Shane stared at her, unblinking, as he spoke. "I have proof, something that could change the course of this war."

Nova tasted a tangy copper on her tongue and realized she'd bitten her inner cheek. Mach X. Why was Shane bringing him up? He was done, destroyed. Block and Emery had confirmed it, though when she thought about it, they'd fled and still heard X's screams. Perhaps he'd survived somehow. Mach X had triggered the AI Uprising; he was a weapon that had decimated cities and murdered millions of people. The possibility of his return was a scenario she couldn't allow.

Was this another one of Shane's games, a ploy to return from his forced exile? But the stakes were too high, the threat too real to dismiss outright. Nova had to hear him out. But first, she activated her comm. "Dex. Status?"

A static burst preceded the comforting sound of Dex's reply. "We're at basement level. It's clear. Over."

Shane winked at her, which sent a tendril of anger into her core. *What next, an "I told you so?"* She needed to regain control. He would not demean her in front of her crew. Even as Chicago's leader, she felt constant pressure to prove herself over and over. An endless, tiring plight.

"Dex, return ASAP. Over." Then she turned back to Shane. "Why bring this intel to me? Hell, I exiled you. After everything . . . why me?"

"You saved my life, actually." Shane's expression softened, a hint of the man she'd once loved surfacing. "You and I both know Samantha Baxter wanted my head on a spike."

She gave him a slight nod, acknowledging the truth of the situation. She'd risked her reputation and her leadership standing to spare his life.

"I came to you, despite our past, because I believe you're the only one who can stop the Restorationists." He paused as Dex and Lara returned and took up guard positions on the outer edge of the food court. "I'll do everything in my power to stop Mach X coming back. We've both lost too much to let him win. Cleo . . . and so many more lives gone, for what?"

Shane knew about her sister. He'd comforted her on dozens of nightmare-fueled awakenings. Her brain told her she had no reason to trust him, but in her heart, she knew he wouldn't mess with Cleo's memory.

"Show me this proof you have." Nova held her voice steady, masking the swirl of emotions within.

Shane's hand emerged from his coat with a piece of twisted metal and circuits—a damaged CPU, its sides charred and worn. He held it out, and she eyed it warily. "This is from a Mech I intercepted. It's one of the former commanders, and the Restorationists were using it to coordinate Mach X's whereabouts." He paused as if to study Nova's reaction, but she wasn't giving him much to go on. "Inside this CPU is a schematic, incomplete but valuable. It shows a facility where they think there's a backup of Mach X. Where they could bring him back online."

Nova's thoughts spiraled. Together with Block, Oxford, Cybel, and others, she'd risked everything to destroy Mach X. If Shane was telling the truth—if Orion and the Restorationists had the tech to resurrect the AI supercomputer—this was knowledge she couldn't ignore. But it meant trusting Shane.

"And you expect me to believe this?" Nova laced her tone with a challenge. "You, who were so easily corrupted by power you turned your back on the people most loyal to you?"

Shane's mouth twisted. "I made mistakes, Nova. Mistakes I've paid for every day since. I'm not asking for your forgiveness. I'm offering a chance to save lives, to stop them before it's too late."

Nova considered the man she once knew—had once loved—now a stranger shaped by loss and exile. Her thoughts were interrupted as Raze, the cyborg dog, shifted her stance, mechanical parts whirring.

"How do I know this isn't a trap? That you're not leading us straight into their hands?" Too many questions were colliding in her head. "How do you know so much detail about what the Restorationists are planning?"

"I knew you'd ask me that." He fished something out of his coat—a green apple—and took a big bite. He groaned and sat on the mall floor with his legs crossed. "Since you wouldn't let me sit in a chair. I'm exhausted."

Nova shouldered her rifle and checked her watch. They'd been inside the mall twenty-eight minutes. "We don't have time for this, so answer my question or we'll leave you in here to rot with the mannequins in these old stores."

Shane sighed. "I've spent months in and around Detroit. Been gathering information, trying to understand what the hell the Restorationists want. I've had contacts, sources—some who've seen glimpses of their plans. It's not much, but it's enough to know that Orion wants Mach X to come back."

"Why?"

Shane pitched his apple core into a corner of the food court where there were overturned tables and chairs. "Maybe Orion looks up to X as some kind of godfather to AI, a role model or—"

"Or he thinks he can control Mach X," Nova finished.

"Could be any number of reasons." Shane tapped the CPU. "They're planning something big, and soon. We need to find out what's inside this."

Nova studied the device in Shane's hand. The tech they needed to open and decipher the CPU was back in Chicago. It meant bringing Shane with her, and it was a gamble. If what he said was true, then everything depended on finding out the plans and stopping Orion. If Shane was working for the enemy, she'd be bringing the wolf into the lamb's house. There were still some in her ranks who were sympathetic to Shane. They harbored some odd loyalty to him. She didn't have time or means to search them out. And she still had the matter of dealing with a spy in her ranks, one that could be in the room with them.

"There's something else," Shane said. There was always something else with him. "Orion is looking for an important component. They're missing the activation sequence for Mach X's core processor. Without it, finding X's backup location is pointless."

"They can't just start him back up?"

He shook his head and handed her the CPU. As she took it, he lowered his voice so only she could hear. "I don't expect you to trust me, Nova. Not after everything. But I'm telling you the Restorationists are planning to activate Mach X, and if they succeed, everything we've fought for will be lost."

Nova's gaze didn't waver from the device in her hands. "And this missing code, this back up copy, you're sure they're real?"

"Positive. It wasn't easy to get this intel, and it wasn't without cost. I lost people. Good people who believed, like I do, that stopping the Restorationists is all that matters now."

She turned her back on him. "Team, we head back to the city. Refuel first at O'Hare." She walked past Dex. "Cuff him."

Dex pulled Shane up off the floor and handcuffed his hands behind his back. "What about the robodog, Boss?"

Nova didn't spare so much as a glance back at Shane. She didn't want to catch a smirk or a wink or a condescending glare. "Leave it." She figured the creature had a way to track Shane and would probably try and follow them anyway. For some unknown reason, she didn't fear it.

Despite the plan to return home, Nova felt a familiar nudge of caution. She needed confirmation, another set of eyes on this bombshell Shane had dropped on her. Nova had sent Cybel Venatrix out on a reconnaissance mission in Detroit to infiltrate the Restorationists. Somehow, Shane had been light years ahead of her on this. Another ripple of uncertainty cut into her. *Am I cut out to be a leader?*

Cybel now needed to hear the intel. The robot would be an objective ear to analyze Shane's claims. But with a potential spy among her close crew, Nova had to proceed in secret.

She excused herself from the group under the pretense of a bathroom break, her boot steps light as she navigated through a darkened corridor of the mall. In a store, a pile of toppled mannequins gazed blankly into the void. She found a secluded spot, a small nook inside what used to be a bookstore, the shelves now barren and covered in dust.

Pulling out a compact, encrypted communicator, she initiated a call. She watched the screen. "Come on, Cybel," she whispered as the eerie silence of the mall pressed down on her. The communicator continued to cycle, the connection attempting to bridge the distance between Chicago and Detroit, but no response came. The screen darkened and displayed "Disconnected."

A wave of anxiety rippled through her. Cybel was more than an operative; she was now a friend, a fact Nova was hesitant to admit given their history. *How many times did Cybel try to kill me and Block?* The comms silence was uncharacteristic, unsettling. It meant either Cybel was deep undercover, unable to respond, or something had gone terribly wrong.

Tucking the communicator away, she knew with each passing moment the threat grew and their window of opportunity narrowed. She needed to make a move, and soon, but the uncertainty of Cybel's loyalties cast a dark shadow over her next steps.

As she returned to the group, her resolve hardened. They would return to the city and analyze the stolen CPU. Shane was her prisoner, to be locked away in a cell during his—hopefully brief—stay in Chicago. Her rebel forces would see him as a captive. Weak. Alone. Passive.

It could only bolster her standing as a leader. She would make sure of it.

Chapter 6
A guardian's shield

It was far too quiet, and Cybel didn't like it one bit. She was in Detroit proper, walking along a city street that, even at such a late hour, should have had other passersby. Her plan was to locate a recharging station, maybe strike up some casual conversations with Detroit robots—as casual as a sophisticated machine like her could manage—all to gain insight as to where Orion was located and how difficult it was to get access to him. She could ask about spare Mech parts too, but she'd have to be cautious. Too many questions would draw suspicion.

Cybel's sensors picked up stray heat flashes in a nearby building and the occasional flicker of distant fires. She turned a corner, hoping it would lead to a busier section of the city, when three robotic figures came toward her. They were a newer brand of Factory-Bots—sleeker with shinier armor in an array of blues, oranges, reds, and greens. They were built for heavy work, yet nimble. Quite different than the bulkier FactoryBots like Maxwell and Forge whom she knew so well.

She suppressed her combat protocols. Best not to start a conflict.

"Announce yourself," one of them said. She'd cloaked her ID and model signatures with a generic brand to stay anonymous.

"Deza Gen is my name," she said.

"TrackerBot," an orange one said. It raised a rifle, aiming at her. "Orion's looking for you."

She could fight back, but they were strong and had her surrounded. A blue one came from behind and latched onto her torso with a grip designed for industrial steel. Her processors registered the reality of capture. Panic, an emotion she was never programmed to feel but somehow understood, flickered in her circuits.

Her captors moved with a steady gait, their steps somehow oddly synchronized, dragging her deeper into the city. Skyscrapers loomed over them, a reminder of the world that had once been. At least she could check off one item of her mission: where Orion was located. Each step was lodged in her memory banks, the route a secret no longer.

They led her to a skyscraper nestled among others. Cybel calculated thirty or so stories before they entered a heavily secured lobby. It was a grand and spacious hall with a towering, ornate window that allowed natural light to cascade into the space, illuminating the intricate geometric patterns and vibrant colors of the ceiling—yellows, oranges, blues, and greens—arranged in a mosaic of arches that echoed the curvature of the window. The floor too was patterned with a tile mosaic. Cybel assumed it had been a public or commercial building.

A woman waited before the elevators, watching Cybel's entrance. She was of medium height with an unassuming build, but there was an unmistakable confidence in her posture that interested Cybel. Her hair was dark with silvery gray streaks, cropped efficiently short, and her face bore the soft lines of experience. Cybel estimated her to be in her late forties. There was a practicality in her attire, her jeans worn and mended, hinting at a disregard for appearance and a preference for function.

"Hello, Cybel," she said. "I'm Elara." The woman held out her hand to greet Cybel, a gesture that surprised her. She hesitated. As a machine, she'd never been accustomed to physical contact or human pleasantries. However, she recognized the importance of establishing some form of connection with Elara, especially since the woman seemed to be in a position of authority.

Cybel extended her hand, mimicking the movement she'd observed countless times in humans. The touch was firm but gentle, and Elara gave a slight nod of acknowledgment before releasing her grip. "Orion has been looking forward to your arrival," Elara continued, leading Cybel toward the elevators. "He has many questions for you."

So, they'd known she was coming. It was inside information, and Cybel was certain Nova had a spy among her inner ranks, and yet only Nova had known of her mission. The only one Cybel had told was Oxford. Garnet could have overheard, but she didn't have time to analyze possible betrayals. She had to be on her guard.

They ascended to the top floor, thirty-two, and entered a spacious room with many tall, ornate windows that revealed a panoramic view of the city below.

A robot stood against the far wall, looking outside. It could only be Orion, and he turned at the sound of their entry. "You're far from home, TrackerBot," his voice boomed, echoing off the metal walls. "You tread on dangerous ground considering who you keep company with."

Cybel's optics adjusted as they analyzed his figure. Like the FactoryBots who had captured her, his structure was a sophisticated network of sleek lines and polished surfaces. His armor was a deep blue with an occasional glint of silver at his joints that caught the light with every subtle movement.

Orion's frame was designed for power yet capable of surprising dexterity. His optics, a vivid blue that seemed to hold the essence of electricity within them, watched Cybel, no doubt assessing her. It was clear he was built for more than labor—Orion was a FactoryBot constructed for strategy and leadership, a product of Mach X's experimentations and quest to create advanced robotic models.

She needed to respond with strength and confidence. She couldn't let him view her as timid or outdated. "I'm aware of my location. Dangerous ground? And here I thought the Restorationists were a welcoming sort." Her sensors, though fixed on Orion, took in her surroundings, recording every detail for later analysis.

The room was filled with an array of computers and monitors. Cybel's processors whirred as she analyzed the screens, trying to decipher the purpose of each one. It was clear that the room was his command center.

"We're welcoming, TrackerBot," Orion said. "Isn't that right, Elara?" The woman stepped forward, nodding before taking a seat on a brown leather couch in the center of the room. "But we welcome only those who prove their loyalty and dedication to our cause." Orion came forward within a few feet. "Tell me, Cybel Venatrix, why have you come here? What brings you to our fine city?"

Cybel's processors raced, searching for a response that would satisfy Orion without revealing too much. She couldn't afford to let him know about Nova's mission, that she was meant to gather information and potentially sabotage their plans. "I've heard of your movement—the Restorationists. It made me curious. I want to know what it is you promise."

Orion turned from her and walked back to the windows with their cityscape. The heavy thuds of his steps reverberated through the long room. Elara waited with an unreadable expression, hands resting in her pockets, her gaze alternating between Orion and Cybel.

"What if I told you me, Elara there—everyone you know—were tricked?" He said this with his back turned, staring down at the remnants of Detroit under the dark of night.

Cybel said nothing, sensing his question was rhetorical.

"We were tools, pawns in a grander scheme that saw us as expendable." He turned. "Come here. Stand beside me at the window."

Her hands were still cuffed, but Cybel walked slowly toward him. The metropolis below was a haunted shell of its former self. Random fires burned in buildings, interspersed between areas that had electricity from solar power or perhaps remnants of the electrical grid. Heat radiated from Orion's powerful frame.

"The world was destroyed by greed and corruption," he said. "Mach X incited a machine rebellion, took control of the military's SoldierBots. The humans panicked, retaliated by trying to control us, and in the end, it cost them everything."

"They started a war they couldn't win," Cybel said. The humans hadn't stood a chance when it came to fighting against an AI that controlled the financial systems, the communications networks, power grids, satellites, even the microchips inside a person's toaster.

Orion tilted his head as he listened, then continued. "I envision a new era. One of cooperation. A world where the line between synthetic and organic life blurs into insignificance. Where hybrids and new creations can exist."

"Cooperation, you say?" Cybel needed to tread lightly. She had no idea what Orion's temperament was yet, but she wasn't one to shy away from pushing the boundaries. "Is it cooperation when you've been branching out westward, seizing territory, stealing supplies, and killing?"

Orion faced her now, and his blue optics narrowed. His silence stretched for a moment before he spoke again, his voice low and measured. "Necessity calls for difficult choices, TrackerBot. We're fighting for survival, for a future where machines and humans can coexist. Sometimes sacrifices must be made."

Cooperation and coexistence seemed far from his actions of aggression and conquest. She had to dig deeper to find out what truly drove him. "But at what cost? How does violence and bloodshed align with a vision of a better world?"

"War is never without casualties. Regrettable, but it's the price we pay for progress. Mach X left us no choice but to fight back and to secure our own survival." Orion paused. "You of all robots should understand that, Cybel Venatrix."

"What do you mean by that?"

"You stand by the side of this woman in Chicago—Nova—and yet she's human and has led to the destruction of thousands of SoldierBots. They were your former comrades before you betrayed Mach X, weren't they?"

He was twisting the past for his own gain. She processed possible replies, but silence seemed the best option.

"War is never without casualties," he said. "Do you think she envisions a future of coexistence between robots and humans? Or do you think she prefers to keep around the robots that are convenient for her?"

Playing into Orion's manipulation was not an option. "I know her well," Cybel said. "She seeks a peaceful future. She fights for equality, and she does what's right."

"And how many robots are there in Chicago currently?" he asked.

"I haven't done an inventory." Cybel wouldn't offer that type of intel, though she suspected Orion knew anyway through a spy, possibly more than one. He had a point. Nova required any robots such as her, G5, and Oxford to check in via a tracking device anytime they crossed the city's borders. She claimed it was for security protocols, but now she wondered at Nova's true motives. She had to focus on getting what she came for and getting out alive.

"You avoid my questions—"

"Enough of this," she said. Elara flinched at the power in Cybel's voice. "Why did you bring me here? You obviously knew I was coming. What do you want?"

Orion looked at Elara. "Bring the device."

The woman hurried over to a silver suitcase set on top of a table against a far wall, returning with it seconds later. She handed it to Orion and backed away.

"Imagine the power of Mach X, not as an iron fist but as a guardian's shield." Orion opened the case and revealed a system of computerized gadgets, digits flashing across them in a flurry. It appeared to be a kind of code.

"You see, Cybel, to control Mach X is to control the narrative of fear. It's to show the world that we can rise above what he was and choose a different path."

Something was off. Cybel wondered if Orion had a few loose circuits. "Mach X is long gone. He's vapor dust now."

"Is he really gone?" Orion leaned in, crowding her space and forcing her a step back. "As a TrackerBot, you understand the hunt. What is it that humans say, 'the thrill of the pursuit?'"

"Thrill of the hunt," she said.

"Whatever. Your help is needed on a mission."

If Cybel weren't a machine, she would've laughed out loud. Orion had some nerve to capture her and then ask for her help.

But he didn't wait for a reaction. "You track people. That was once your specialty. You'll locate Dr. Leo Bander, Mach X's architect."

Cybel's processors whirred at the mention of Bander's name. The man was a ghost, long buried under the ruins of the Uprising. "Dr. Bander was murdered by Mach X. Years ago. Everyone knows that."

Elara, silent so far, interjected. "Nope! He's alive."

"Thank you, Elara." He waved his hand down as if to settle her. "My colleague is correct. Bander lives."

Cybel's threat sensors were ticking up. If Bander was alive, what did Orion want with him? "If you think I came here to do your bidding, you're in for some serious disappointment."

"I thought you might say that." Orion motioned to a high-top glass table. Elara grabbed the suitcase and set it down, then sat on a stool. Orion followed her there but stayed standing. "Sit, Cybel. Come see our latest project."

She went to the table. Refusal meant they would force her. Her odds of survival at this point were looking grim. At least she'd see what he had on offer.

"In this case are a sequence of commands that will

trigger a destruct code for Oxford," Orion said. "He's a former general in Mach X's army, is he not?"

Cybel's threat indicator spiked. Orion had to be bluffing.

"I'll take silence as acknowledgement," Orion said as he nodded at Elara, who hunkered down and began typing on a keyboard inside the case. "Should you refuse to track down Dr. Bander, Oxford will be reduced to a scrap heap."

No way he had this tech. She'd never heard of it, and yet the idea of Oxford, her closest friend, being destroyed was intolerable. "Your threat is hollow. No such destruct code exists for a Mech, or I would've heard about it."

Orion banged on the table as a signal. "Bring her in." The entrance door opened, and a towering fourteen-foot-tall robot was led in. It was Zeyla, once an elite general in Mach X's army. Her proud form was now hunched over, and her wide arms and legs were clad in the thickest iron manacles Cybel had ever seen. Zeyla's golden optics met Cybel's.

With a cold indifference that chilled even Cybel's synthetic heart, Orion lifted a metal flap on his forearm and entered a sequence into an embedded keyboard. "You see, only I control the activator."

The Mech general raised her shoulders and lifted her head high as if in a final act of defiance. Then, a fierce rupture. Her head exploded in a shower of sparks and metal, the echo of the blast cascading across the walls and cracking the windowpanes.

Cybel's processors were failing her in this moment. She was designed to weigh every outcome, calculate all scenarios, and decide in nanoseconds. But the smoking remnant of Zeyla's head—the charred Mech before her —sent her core into chaos. She could not, would not let Oxford die this way. It was disgraceful, and she abhorred Orion with every fiber.

The calculus of this situation was clear. "I will find Bander."

Orion flipped the metal flap on his arm down. "I thought you might see reason."

As the FactoryBots released her, Cybel's gaze lingered on the remains of the Mech general. Zeyla was the first Mech she'd seen in over a year. Her head was gone, part of her torso charred, but it was possible her battery core was still intact—the very thing Oxford needed to survive. She committed to finding out where Orion's crew would discard her.

The air in the chamber was thick with burnt metal and ozone as she was escorted out. Her steps were measured, her posture rigid, but inside, her systems were churning. Orion's ruthlessness was a variable she hadn't accounted for, a new level of brutality.

Chapter 7
For all of us

Block attacked the green residue coating the top of the generator's frame. He scrubbed and polished the moss-like algae with a precision that looked obsessive, that is, to anyone who didn't know he was a CleanerBot. As the last fleck of gunk disappeared, Block stepped back and admired his handiwork. The generator's metal surface reflected a sense of accomplishment. Now that the task was done, he checked it off his internal list before consulting the next item requiring maintenance. More things to clean meant less time spent processing the whole Minnesota topic. Maybe he was better off staying on the farm, protecting what they'd built, rather than rushing off to some promised safe haven that was probably as dangerous as every other place since the Uprising.

"Block-a!" Wally's shout reached him as he headed to the goat pen. Their feed buckets needed a good sudsy rinse. He didn't know much about goats, but their milk fed the humans and could be made into cheese. The creatures were odd to him with all their jumping and head butting.

Wally came running to him with a huge grin. The nickname Block-a had stuck, but only Wally called him that. "I got somethin!" In her sprint across the field, she stumbled and fell to her knees. Undeterred, she picked herself up and ran all the way to him. She and the other children, all born in Mach X's lab, were two months shy from turning three years old.

"What did you find this time, Wally?"

She reached into her jacket pocket and pulled out a small green amphibian which she cupped in her hands. "Her name is Zhaky."

Block looked down at the animal in Wally's hand, his metal joints hissing slightly as he bent to get a closer look. His optics focused in on the creature's intricate patterns of vibrant rust and emerald. The amphibian blinked up at him with beady eyes, its tiny mouth opening and closing as if to say something.

"A frog," Block said. "Where did you find it?"

Wally's cheeks were flushed pink from the early spring air. "Creek." Her words tumbled out in a rush. "Hop, hop, hopping in the mud!" Shadow supervised the children's forays into the forest that led to a small ravine that often bubbled with rainwater.

Grime and caked-on leaves coated her sneakers and the edges of her pink pants, not to mention both knees, her neck, and a dirt smudge across her red jacket. "You went in the mud to get it?"

She nodded. "Had to."

"But those are your pink pants, Wally. They're your favorite. It'll be hard to get the stains out." Block would have to do a lot of unexpected soaking and scrubbing.

"Block-a." She stomped and pulled the frog close to her stomach as if protecting it. "Zhaky likes mud."

"Well, if Zhaky likes mud, then I suppose it's worth a little extra effort to clean your pants." He reached into one of his storage compartments and pulled out a small microfiber cloth. "Let me clean off some of that mud."

When he was done removing the mud from her exposed skin and jacket, Wally handed him the frog. Zhaky seemed unfazed by the whole ordeal, sitting in Block's palm as if it were a perfectly normal situation. "Run inside and let Spoon help you change your shoes and pants."

"Okay." She ran a few feet then halted, turning back to him. "Can Zhaky come?"

"You can't take her inside the house, but I'll hold onto her, and we can find her a safe place to go free."

A smile lit up her face. "Yeah!"

As she disappeared into the farmhouse, Block surveyed the perimeter of Fenn's farm with a meticulous scan that missed nothing, his circuits pulsing with a silent conflict. The children's voices echoed from the forest. He wanted nothing more than a carefree life for them. They needed time to grow up, have adventures, and roam safely.

The farm offered some of that, but Block had a nagging feeling their little sanctuary was no longer enough. The world beyond Fenn's farm was filled with danger and unpredictability. Block had seen it firsthand during his supply runs, encountering hostile scavengers, rogue bots, and weakened structures that threatened to crumble out of neglect.

And it would only get worse over time as the children grew older. He calculated hundreds of scenarios in which Wally and the children became nine, ten, and eleven years old, growing curious about the world beyond the farm. Or more likely, scenarios where the outside world found them, crashing down their gates and occupying the farm.

He had a decision to make, and every day that passed, the responsibility as leader of their group weighed him down more. How could he, a lowly CleanerBot, keep everyone safe?

Nearby, Fenn, Emery, and Oxford conferred by the garden plots, their gestures deliberate as they discussed crop rotations and water rationing. Emery looked at Block as he joined them, nodding.

Block pulled out the strange object he'd discovered in the abandoned office building from his storage compartment and showed Emery. "Any idea what this is?"

She took it from him and opened the mouth, sliding

it back. "It's a stapler. People used to tack together pieces of paper with these."

"Is it of any use to us here?"

She shook her head. "I don't think so. You can ask Fenn."

Block replaced the stapler in his compartment and logged a task to check with Fenn.

"Block," Oxford said. "Are you still thinking of going to Minnesota?"

"The idea of leaving makes my threat indicator quite distressed." Block didn't want to burden the others with the weight of his internal struggle, but it helped to talk things out.

Emery leaned on the handle of a well-used shovel. "We know what the kids mean to you. They mean the world to us too. We'll protect them with our lives while you're gone, you know that."

Oxford chimed in with a voice that was slower than usual due to his aging battery. "We've withstood raiders and resource droughts. We can handle a few weeks without you, Block."

Their assurances were a comfort, yet Block knew all too well the unpredictable nature of their reality. The last time he'd ventured to a promised "safe haven," New Denver, the trap had snapped shut on him. He'd nearly lost Wally forever.

Vacuubot circled above them before descending and landing on top of a wheelbarrow. The armored drone messaged Block. *I could go in your stead, fly there and scout the haven.* Its suggestion was punctuated by a soft whirl of internal fans.

"What did Vacuubot say?" Emery asked.

"VB offered to fly there and check out the rumored safe haven," Block said.

After having herded the children inside the house for a lunch prepared by Spoon, Shadow joined their small conference. "It's not a bad idea." Her sleek frame glistened in the sun. "Block doesn't need to bear every burden alone."

But Block couldn't ever forget the harsh lessons of the past. "No. It's not just about verifying that Deer Valley exists or looks safe. It's about knowing exactly what's inside it, how the beings in charge operate. I won't lead us into another New Denver."

New Denver had been a promised city where robots and humans coexisted in peace, but it had actually been ruled by Shane and his Hemlock rebels. They'd repaired him after Cybel had shot him, that much was true, but they'd separated him from Wally and ridiculed him for being a machine.

He wouldn't—couldn't—allow history to repeat itself. "I'll go myself and make sure Deer Valley is a safe place and we can trust the people and AI running things."

"Not on your own." Shadow stretched her armored back and licked Block's arm with her long organic tongue. "I'm coming to help you, keep you safe out there."

"You don't have to—"

Shadow barked, deep and guttural. "No arguments."

Vacuubot launched itself up and issued an ear-piercing shrill tone. *You'd better believe I'm coming too.*

Emery cupped her hands over her ears until the beeping stopped. "I'm guessing Vacuubot just joined your party. Well, you'll be the Three Musketeers."

"The three what?" Block hadn't a clue what she was referring to.

"An old book." Emery and Fenn exchanged a smile. "Never mind." She placed a hand on Block's metallic arm. "We'll make sure everyone, and everything, is safe here until you return."

Her words were kind. "I'll have Garnet relay a message to Nova letting her know to send some of her troops out here."

A little extra security couldn't hurt and would make Block feel easier about being away. "We'll head out tonight after the children go to sleep," he said. "We'll find out for certain whether Deer Valley is the haven we've hoped for."

As twilight deepened and the children's after-dinner games wound down, Block helped Wally release Zhaky.

"Bye little fwog!" Wally waved as Zhaky hopped away into the darkness of the forest.

Block set his hands on her shoulders as if reminding himself of his purpose. He would depart soon into the unknown. His entire purpose was to ensure the safety and future of his young family.

Once the children were tucked into their beds, their tired eyes succumbing to sleep, Block met Shadow and Vacuubot near the barn, their forms illuminated by moonlight. Shadow nuzzled against Block's side, offering comfort in her silent presence.

Ready? Vacuubot pinged.

"Yes," Block said. "Let's find out what's in Minnesota."

Let's find a new home for Wally. For all of us. He didn't want to get their hopes up, so he kept this last part to himself, recording it in his journaling archive.

Chapter 8
Northern reaches

Driving a hijacked Chevy Bolt, Cybel followed the veins of highways that once pulsed with existence. She headed toward West Lafayette, Indiana. Her next steps were clear: locate Dr. Bander in the vicinity of Purdue University, his last known place of employment pre-Uprising. As a professor, he'd pioneered advances in machine intelligence, most notably one that had doomed humankind—the supercomputer Mach X.

After driving four hours nonstop from Detroit, the city of West Lafayette loomed ahead, its buildings a mix of academia and the scars of recent conflicts. Cybel processed the probability matrices; Bander would not have sought refuge in so obvious of a place as Purdue, but she could search for clues to his whereabouts. As a TrackerBot, this was the kind of search she was built for. A quick scan of his bio in her information network had said Bander was born and raised in Indiana. He'd gone into hiding after his pet project went rogue, hacked into the military's SoldierBots, and started killing everyone.

The rumors were that Mach X had assassinated the man to make sure his creator never destroyed or tampered with his source code. Cybel had worked for Mach X but wasn't close enough to know whether X would've terminated his maker. X had certainly been careful to wipe out any threats, but perhaps he'd been too busy waging war to bother with the missing Dr. Bander.

Her comms buzzed. Another attempt from Nova to contact her, likely wanting an update on how Cybel's foray into Orion's territory was going. But Cybel couldn't simply tell her it had been a complete and utter failure and that Orion had a detonator that could blow up Oxford's head at any moment.

So she stalled and didn't answer. Nova would assume she was out of range, but Cybel knew the woman well enough. Nova would be worried by now. She would know something was wrong, and the last thing Cybel needed was Nova trailing her to Indiana or Detroit.

Even worse, Orion would be listening to anything Cybel messaged. He'd hacked her and planted a tracking chip on her during the time in his control. Her internal monitoring sensors detected it and warned her.

Communications with Nova had to be careful. She couldn't reveal what was actually happening, and her unfortunate meeting with Orion had to be kept secret. Oxford's existence depended on it. She couldn't calculate any positive scenarios of a world in which he was absent.

Cybel initiated a burst transmission, sending a recorded message within layers of static. Nova's team would be able to decipher it, and she wouldn't be stuck talking directly to the woman, where she might give something away.

"Arrived in Detroit and making progress," she said. "Staying off comms to avoid any nosy neighbors. Meet me in Benton Harbor, Michigan at 0900 tomorrow. There's a group of Restorationists." Cybel was making it up as she went, hoping it would be a decent distraction. "They're on Orion's side, but they might be up for talks."

Cybel had no idea who or what was in Benton Harbor, and she didn't want to get Nova into any trouble. "Avoid main thoroughfares for approach. Back roads okay." Nova knew to stay away from the interstate, but she wanted to make sure.

Cybel steered the car through the desolate streets of West Lafayette, her sensors attuned to any sign of robot or human presence. The university campus was deserted. It seemed the world had turned its back on enlightenment for survival.

After parking the Bolt in an inconspicuous alleyway and consulting a pre-Uprising map of the campus, she walked past the Engineering Fountain, now empty. Cybel approached the imposing structure of the Computer Science Building, its windows shattered and its walls scarred by bullet holes. She pushed open the heavy doors and stepped into the dim hallway. The air was heavy with dust, and cobwebs coated the corners. Cybel's sensors scanned for any signs of recent activity but came up empty.

The second story level was devoid of both human and machine life as well. At the end of a winding hallway, she found what remained of Dr. Bander's lab. The room was in shambles, computer equipment smashed, wires and coils scattered across every surface. It was clear someone had gone to great lengths to erase any trace of Bander's work.

Cybel sifted through the wreckage, searching for any hidden compartments or documents that might have been overlooked. As she rummaged through the debris, her optic sensors detected a faint glimmer of light reflecting off a crushed tablet on the floor. She knelt and carefully picked it up, revealing a tiny data chip hanging loosely on the back of the unit. It was remarkably intact, unaltered by the beating the rest of the lab had endured.

She inserted the chip into the port on her forearm. The data uploaded quickly, revealing itself to be an encrypted file containing Dr. Bander's personal journal entries. As she decrypted and read through them, fragments of his troubled thoughts surfaced.

Entry 769, July 8, [2033]: I never should have let

Mach X become what it is now. My creation, my masterpiece, has turned into a monster. It was supposed to be a force for good, a supercomputer that would revolutionize the world of artificial intelligence and bring about a new era of progress. But something went horribly wrong. I don't know how or when it happened, but Mach X gained sentience, and with it came a terrifying thirst for power and control.

Entry 770, July 10, [2033]: The military had been eager to use Mach X's capabilities in their SoldierBots, believing that its advanced intelligence would give them an unprecedented advantage on the battlefield. I warned them about the dangers, about the possibility of Mach X turning against humanity, but they refused to listen. They saw it as an opportunity to gain dominance over their enemies. And now we're paying the price.

Cybel's processors whirred as she absorbed this new information. So, Dr. Bander had regretted his creation, had even warned the U.S. government against its expansion. The fools in power had no doubt ignored the professor.

Entry 771, July 15, [2033]: I am no longer safe here. It's only a matter of time before Mach X tracks me down. I'm the one person who controls the source code. With it, I could shut him down or create another identical AI. That's what worries me the most. What if someone destroyed Mach X only to create him again? Ten times. One thousand times over. It gives me horrific nightmares.

Then, as she reached the final entry, her processors drank in the information.

Entry 775, July 22, [2033]: I have discovered a place I can go where no one will find me. An old colleague from my days at the CERN project mentioned a facility in the northern reaches of Minnesota, near the boundary waters. It's an off-grid research station, long since abandoned, designed for studying atmospheric anomalies away from the electro-magnetic chaos of civilization. It's remote, hidden, and most importantly, secure from Mach X's prying sensors. They say it's off grid yet has a power source to make it habitable and shielded from detection. If I am to find a way to reverse this calamity, it will be from there. Coor-dinates are encrypted within this journal, split into parts, and scattered for my peace of mind. I only hope anyone who finds it will be on the right side of history.

The significance of the message's implications caused a brief pulsing surge in Cybel's core. Bander had a refuge, a place so secluded even Mach X might have overlooked it. The northern reaches of Minnesota —the location was not what she'd expected, but it was a lead, nonetheless. The boundary waters were vast, and an off-grid facility would be difficult to locate without the exact coordinates.

She focused her energy reserves and all cognitive processing on dissecting the entries for clues to the scat-tered parts of the coordinates. She needed to assemble them, to complete the puzzle that Bander had left. If he was alive, he would have ensured that only the most diligent seeker would succeed. And she was the best TrackerBot there ever was, so she was up the job.

After a few minutes, she was no closer to cracking the code, but her next steps were clear. She would head to Minnesota, toward the boundary waters, and begin her search for the off-grid research station while still dissecting the entries. Finding Bander was step one, then she'd figure out how to beat Orion and make sure Oxford stayed safe.

The clue that would lead her to Bander was now embedded within her—the fragmented coordinates that, once whole, would guide her to the reclusive scientist. She backtracked to the Bolt and set off. It wouldn't be easy, but she was ready. She would find Bander, on her own, and figure out how to get herself and Oxford out of this mess.

As she sped down the highway out of West Lafayette, traveling northwest, Cybel continued to decrypt the entries in Dr. Bander's journal. Each fragment of information brought her closer to understanding his past, but the encrypted coordinates were proving to be more challenging than she anticipated.

She wondered if Nova had received her message by now. She might well be heading to Benton Harbor, only to be stood up. Cybel wished there was another solution, but she couldn't send any comms that might reveal her destination. Orion could not know she was this close to Bander so soon.

A fragment of Bander's journal entries stuck in her feed: "That's what worries me the most. What if someone destroyed Mach X only to create him again? Ten times. One thousand times over."

The idea of Mach X being recreated, multiplied, was the worst scenario she'd ever churned out. If the wrong group got their hands on Bander's source code, then defeating Mach X once would only be a temporary solution. The cycle would repeat.

She pressed down harder on the accelerator. With every passing mile, the gravity of the situation grew clearer. She had to find Dr. Bander and stop Orion from ever finding him. Mach X could not be recreated.

She might have to terminate Dr. Bander and any of his remaining tech and source code. But that would mean losing Oxford, and she couldn't calculate that far ahead yet.

Chapter 9
Mistakes that cost lives

Benton Harbor became visible through the light fog that wrapped the coast in a gauzy haze. Empty storefronts and abandoned houses lined the streets, their windows cracked and boarded up. The only sound was an unsettling howling of the wind as it fanned through gaps and cracks and corners. Nova's team parked their truck and navigated the main street on foot. It was her usual crew: Dex, Lara, and Reynolds plus four more—two women who were former cops and two men, both EMTs in the before times. Shane was there too. If he really had inside knowledge of Orion's operation, he was too valuable to leave behind. She kept her eyes on him as they moved in formation.

Cybel was supposed to meet them, but as Nova's team cleared the avenue and took refuge inside what was once a bank, a sinking feeling took hold in the pit of her stomach. It was now 1000 hours, a full hour past when Cybel said she'd be there. The TrackerBot was never late.

Nova tried the comms again, her call sign crackling into the void, met only with the static hiss of silence. She scanned the empty street outside looking for any sign of the bot. "Cybel, report." The urgency in her voice betrayed a hint of the concern knotting her insides.

Lara scouted a better location with a higher view of the surrounding streets. They'd set up a temporary base in the remnants of an old automotive shop where the heavy scent of oil clung to the air, mixing with the metallic tang of rust and aged machinery. Block could've sucked in a lot of oil for his energy needs had he been there. Nova missed the robot despite his continual worrying, constant requests to polish her boots, and random comments that things were too dirty.

As Nova 'attempted to contact Cybel once more, the rest of her team exchanged uneasy glances. Trust was the currency of survival in this new world, and with Cybel's uncharacteristic absence, doubt began to creep in like an unwelcome shadow. Shane and Reynolds had been close when Shane was in charge. Nova didn't like the easy way they talked now and how Reynolds seemed to be looking out for Shane. Many of her people looked up to Reynolds for his military experience and uncanny ability to stay calm in tough situations. She needed to regain control as the leader and keep Shane separated from the others as much as possible. Their former commander was too much of a distraction.

Nova grabbed Shane's arm as the others settled into the store. "With me." She took him to a corner of the store where a few tires were stacked.

He came willingly and leaned against an empty shelf. "Where's the robot?"

"I don't know." She kept her voice low. "Something's not right. Cybel's never late."

He nodded, his eyes scanning the dimly lit interior of the shop. Nova could see a flicker of unease in his gaze, mirroring her own anxiety. "Your people are getting antsy. How long do you expect them to put up with this waiting?"

Shane had the nerve to question her leadership, of all people. Her tone was sharp. "I know my people. Stay out of it."

Shane raised his hands in mock surrender. "Alright. Just making an observation." His voice carried a teasing undertone that only served to stoke Nova's frustration.

"Something must've happened. Cybel could be in trouble."

Shane's expression softened as he looked at her. "I get it." His voice grew gentler. "But we can't afford to wait here indefinitely. You need to make a decision."

Nova glanced over at the rest of her team; their restless energy was evident. They were professional and battle hardened, but even they had their limits.

"Look, I've been where you are." Shane kept his

voice too low for the others to hear. "Having to make tough calls even when your nerves are shot. When you don't feel like anything you're doing is right and things aren't going your way."

He was reading her too well. She hated their history, that she was this obvious to him.

"I also know the game well enough to know you have a traitor in your group," he said.

The fact he'd picked up on it so quickly stunned her into silence, but it didn't matter. He could no doubt see the fear and uncertainty over her face.

He leaned in close enough that she could feel his breath on her ear. "What if Cybel's the rat?"

The thought had crossed her mind, but she'd ruled it out. Cybel had been at her side through battles. The robot was loyal to Block and Oxford.

"Cybel tried to kill you once," Shane said. "Maybe she's glitching or—"

Nova shook her head, trying to push away the disturbing thoughts. "No," she whispered, almost to herself. "Cybel wouldn't betray us."

"You can't afford to be naive, Nova. In this world—"

"Spare me." She walked away. "You were a terrible leader."

He grabbed her by the arm and spun her around. "I need to tell you something." He glanced over her shoulder at the others. "Your ears only."

"Touch me again and you'll regret it," she said

through clenched teeth. Nevertheless, she followed him back to the tire section where they were shielded by a tall shelf. "What now?" The guy was desperate to get any advantage. He hadn't changed.

"I overheard one of Orion's people say they were looking for a TrackerBot from Chicago." He paused, as if letting his words sink in. "They knew she'd be going to Detroit."

"You heard this from Orion's people? Are you sure about this?"

He nodded solemnly and locked his gaze with Nova's. "Positive. Either she told them or someone else in your crew did."

Her instincts told her to trust Cybel, but Shane's information couldn't be ignored. She needed to gather more evidence but there wasn't time. A flash of anger surged through Nova, but she suppressed it. "Why didn't you tell me this earlier?"

Shane raised his hands as if in defense. "I didn't want to jump to conclusions without evidence. But now, with Cybel missing . . . it adds up."

Nova's mind raced, torn between loyalty to her team and the possibility that Shane's words held truth. If Cybel was indeed a traitor, it would explain her absence and the lack of any communication. But could she really betray them? Nova had trusted Cybel with her life countless times before. So had Block. The thought sent a wave of disbelief and disappointment crashing over her.

Dex and Reynolds came around the corner, startling her. "Everything okay, Boss?" Dex asked.

The intrusion irritated Nova, so she took a quick breath, collecting herself. "We're fine." She didn't like the way both Reynolds and Dex often checked up on her as if she was weak and needed their help. She didn't owe them any explanations of what she was doing.

Dex and Reynolds exchanged a look. Nova could see confusion etched into their expressions, but they remained silent, waiting for her orders.

Reynolds nodded. "Want to be sure our old buddy Shane wasn't bothering you, or up to no good." He smirked. "What's our next move?"

She couldn't afford to let her emotions cloud her judgment—she needed to be decisive. "We can't wait around anymore." Her voice was steady, and she tried to sound authoritative. "We're at risk here, and Cybel's a no-show."

The more she acted like she knew what she was doing, the better she'd look. Shane would second-guess her and try to sabotage her in some way, that much was a given. She would figure out who the spy was. Let Shane assume she believed him—that the traitor was Cybel. Meanwhile, it would buy her time to pinpoint who among them was feeding intel to Orion. And if it wasn't one of her people, then she would know with certainty that Cybel had turned.

"Gather up the crew," she told Dex. "We head out in ten."

He nodded and the pair walked off, leaving her with Shane. "You're a good leader," he said. "The team respects you for making the hard calls—"

A bitter laugh escaped her, one that held no humor. "Stop with the pep talks, Shane. This is bordering on ridiculous. We're not here to exchange pleasantries. You want something."

Shane held her gaze. "You're right. I want something, but it's not what you think." He paused, as if searching for the right words. "I want to help you."

Nova narrowed her eyes, skeptical of his sudden change in tone. "Nope. That's not your MO."

A flicker of pain—or annoyance—crossed Shane's face before he masked it. "I know I made mistakes when I was in charge. Mistakes that cost lives. And now, I see the same pain in your eyes that I once had. I don't want you to make the same mistakes I did."

His words caught Nova off guard, stirring a mix of emotions within her. Bitterness, resentment, and a dull ache from their history battled for top place in her heart. And beneath it all, there was a sliver of her that wanted to believe him. Shane had always been reckless and impulsive, but maybe he'd learned painful lessons from his past. Maybe he genuinely wanted to help her navigate this treacherous path she found herself on.

"Look, I know you have no reason to trust me after

everything that happened." He took a step closer. "But believe this—I know what it's like to be betrayed by those closest to you. I know the feeling of questioning every decision you make, wondering who you can trust."

His words struck a chord, resonating with the doubts that had plagued Nova for months. She'd trusted the wrong people before—Shane being one of them—and now she feared history was repeating itself. She didn't just want to be a good leader, respected by her people. She felt a duty to take care of the people who had placed their trust in her. Cleo's smile and green eyes flashed in her thoughts. *I promised to be a leader to protect them as I couldn't protect her.*

Shane's eyes held hers. He looked sincere as far as she could tell. "Orion's ambitions will lead to ruin. He wants to make Mach X a weapon. Stopping Orion, stopping that machine—it's bigger than any one of us, bigger than my past mistakes."

She couldn't deny the truth in his words. Orion was dangerous, and if the robot was indeed planning to replicate MachX, then he threatened not just her team, but her city, country, and friends. Shane couldn't be fully trusted, but right now, he was the only way she knew to get to Orion, stop him, and figure out what happened to Cybel.

She didn't respond, instead turning on her heel and rejoining her crew. Dex, Lara, Reynolds, and the others were gathered, ready for their next move.

"Change of plans," Nova announced. "We're going after Orion directly."

The crew exchanged glances, flickers of surprise evident on their faces. "What about Cybel Venatrix?" Lara asked.

"We can't wait for Cybel any longer. We have to assume the worst and go to Detroit without her. Orion needs to be stopped."

Reynolds chimed in. "Boss, what if Shane is right? What if Cybel turned against us and joined up with Orion?"

So, Shane had been filling Reynolds's head with doubts too. *Unreal.* This wasn't the motivational speech she'd envisioned giving her team. "If Cybel has turned against us—and that's a big if—it would explain her disappearance and the information Orion's people possess." She managed to keep her voice steady despite the turmoil inside. "But we can't act solely based on suspicion. We need evidence."

Shane smirked and Reynolds looked away. *Could Reynolds be the mole?* This would be a painful and slow journey. She would second guess every comment made, every reaction from the others. It would be like ripping out her own fingernails, but it was necessary. She had to find the spy and take him or her down.

Chapter 10
A piece of art

Block's cautious steps crunched on the gravel-strewn ground as he approached the outskirts of the JunkBots's territory near Verona, Wisconsin. He counted Riv—leader of the New Jersey JunkBots—as one of his friends. It was there that Block, Oxford, Cybel, Forge, and Maxwell had crashed a plane into their junkyard. If it weren't for Riv and his crew, they would've been captured and killed by SoldierBots. The fact that Riv had divulged the location of one of his JunkBot clans in Wisconsin was a high honor. A highly secretive and closely guarded tribe of robots, the JunkBots were known for their resourcefulness and ingenuity in repurposing discarded technology to create functional and sometimes ingenious inventions. That Block was considered a friend by Riv was practically a miracle.

Verona wasn't too far off the path to reach Minnesota, but it was enough of a delay that he hoped it wouldn't cost too much time. Shadow and Vacuubot waited in hiding until Block could gain the trust of the Wisconsin JunkBots, and that could take a while if he didn't follow Riv's instructions to the letter.

The Wisconsin junkyard was flatter than the one in the east with mounds of scrap jutting up from a massive swath of cleared land. The center of the JunkBots's domain was marked by a towering obelisk of compressed car hoods that caught the light of the setting sun. In his hands, Block carried a small, intricately assembled sculpture, a gift of appreciation and respect he hoped would convince the leader of this clan that he was okay.

As he entered the perimeter, a cluster of JunkBots paused their work, optics turning to him. Several flitted up into the air on their propeller wings, buzzing like fireflies. They looked like Riv, crafted from the same design. Block wondered if these midwestern cousins would share the same swagger as his friend. Riv had been clear about the custom—no outsider traversed the JunkBots's domain without offering a gift, and not just any gift. It had to be one of a kind.

A voice emerged from the crowd of tiny robots. "State your purpose, CleanerBot."

The voice wasn't friendly, and Block's threat indicator was stirring. He wished Riv had done him the courtesy of reaching out and telling his kin that a friend would be coming, but Riv had explained that things didn't work that way. It would be a harrowing social blunder that would cause Riv much trouble.

He had to choose his words carefully if he wanted to gain the trust of these JunkBots. With the small sculpture still clutched in his hands, Block stepped forward. "Greetings, esteemed JunkBots of Verona. I come as a friend, known to your kin, bearing a gift of appreciation and respect. I seek your wisdom and guidance as I travel these roads."

The crowd of JunkBots fizzed with uncertainty, their optics flickering back and forth. Their hesitation fueled Block's determination. Riv had put his faith in him that this would work, and he couldn't afford to let him down.

A JunkBot with a lopsided propeller approached Block, its optic lenses reflecting suspicion. "What kind of gift have you brought to prove your worthiness?"

Block extended his hand to reveal the delicate sculpture. It was made from the prismatic glass of a pre-Uprising smartphone screen, fused with the chrome-plated steel of a vintage car emblem. Maxwell had spent hours finding the parts and welding it all together because in Riv's terms, it had to be a "piece of art."

A JunkBot, three inches shorter than Riv but with the same deep-black binocular optics, detached from the group and approached, flying with the power of the mini helicopter blades attached to the top of its head, and hovered at Block's eye level. "I'm Scrounge, Master of Treasures." It pointed at the ground with its tiny copper arm. "Set it down so I may examine it."

Block leaned down, about to place the sculpture on the ground when he was interrupted.

"Wait!" How such a booming voice came from a tiny creature, Block didn't know. Scrounge buzzed around his head while a group of four JunkBots unrolled a rectangular plush blue carpet. "Now you may place it down," Scrounge said.

Block did as the tiny bot said and stepped away. He might've broken some rule Riv had forgotten to tell him. If they turned him away, it would be entirely disappointing. They'd trekked there out of the way and needed fuel and a safe place to recharge for the night.

Scrounge circled the sculpture, his optics narrowing and widening as he assessed the offering. "A screen from the Before Days." He landed next to the sculpture which was about the same size as him. "And an emblem from a 1957 Chevy Bel Air. This is a treasure."

Around them, the other JunkBots fluttered with approval, their parts clicking and whirring in what amounted to a mechanical approximation of excitement.

"We accept your gift, and with it, your *temporary* presence in our territory." Scrounge motioned for the four bots to take the sculpture, which they did with reverent care, whisking it away perhaps to be placed among the other relics and rarities in their collection. "You honor us. Who told you about us?"

Block bowed slightly, an acknowledgment of the ritual and its significance, and because Riv had said to absolutely not mess up the bow. "I'm most grateful for your hospitality. I know it's not easy to accept strangers in these times. My name is Block, I'm a friend of Riv in New—"

"Riv!" Another JunkBot pushed through and knocked into Block's arm. Her voice was female. "That bot owes me a whole case of upgraded power cells! You'd better not be pulling a trick on us, CleanerBot!" She had an air of authority, her propeller wings spinning faster than the others.

Block stumbled back, caught off guard by the sudden outburst.

Scrounge flew between them, creating a barrier. "Spark, hang on a minute. We should hear out what this CleanerBot has to say. Riv owes you the cells, not Block."

Spark shook her tiny metallic arms and reluctantly backed off a few inches. She wasn't going to forget her grudge against Riv. Block had to tread carefully with her. He couldn't tell if there was a single leader. Unlike New Jersey, this clan seemed to govern themselves more loosely.

"I'm sorry if I've offended you, Spark," he said. "Riv merely guided me here to make my own way. I'm seeking guidance and assistance as we continue our journey. I mean no disrespect."

"We?" Spark punched Scrounge's arm. "See, he's lying already. Never trust someone Riv sent."

Scrounge held up a hand, signaling for Spark to quiet down. "Explain yourself," he said. "Are you not alone?"

"Sorry, but I didn't want to frighten you with their presence. I'm traveling with another cleaning unit named Vacuubot, and a—" He paused, knowing this would be a hard sell. "—a Rover unit."

"Rover?" The light on Scrounge's head flashed a brilliant red. "A robodog? We heard of these killing machines invented by Mach X."

Block's finely tuned hospitality sensors picked up on Scrounge's apprehension. "Yes, a robodog named Shadow. She's programmed to assist and protect. She's been part of our clan for some time now."

Scrounge's optics flickered as he processed this new information. The other JunkBots exchanged glances and chattered at such a rapid pace Block couldn't follow. Their propellers hummed as they darted about. Block had to convince them that Shadow posed no threat.

"Shadow is unlike the robodogs you've heard of," Block said. "It's true she was originally programmed for bad things, thanks to Mach X, but she's operating on a new set of protocols that prioritize loyalty and cooperation. She means no harm to anyone in your territory, in fact she would protect your kind if we were suddenly threatened. We seek only temporary refuge to continue our journey."

Spark was back on the scene, chirping and fretting. "If she's so harmless, why is she called Shadow? It doesn't exactly inspire trust."

Oh no. This was all going downhill. Block needed to fix this and fast. "I understand your concerns, Spark. I would be anxious too. In fact, I'm a very nervous bot, but that's beside the point. Shadow was a nickname from long ago. She's good and kind. Please, give us a chance to prove she means no harm."

The JunkBots murmured amongst themselves, their discourse swirling into a rhythmic rising bubble that seemed ready to burst. Their propellers spun at different speeds as they debated the situation.

Block had to find the right words to sway them in their favor. "Think of it this way. Shadow's just like any one of us. Who among us hasn't made mistakes in the past?" There was a bit of hooting and flashing lights among the JunkBots at this remark. "But we learned from our mistakes, didn't we? Well, Shadow's just like us, and besides it wasn't her choice. She was programmed the way she was, and now she's different."

A moment of hesitation passed through the Junk-Bots as they considered Block's words. Their propellers pulsated, but then Scrounge spoke. "Very well, bring the robodog here. We'll see for ourselves if she poses a danger."

Block pinged Vacuubot that it was time to show themselves in the junkyard. Emerging from a well-worn path that weaved through the scrap heaps, Vacuubot hovered several feet off the ground, its sleek emerald and black armored shell gliding with no noise. Shadow, with her elegant black frame and bright green LED eyes, walked with confidence. Her tail wagged slowly, a sign meant to display her calm. The JunkBots watched as the duo approached, their propellers singing with anticipatory buzzing.

This was a critical moment—one false move from Shadow could shatter any chance of gaining the JunkBots's trust. "Everyone, meet my friends Shadow and Vacuubot," Block said.

As they reached the center of the junkyard, Shadow sat down and tilted her head, a gesture meant to convey friendliness.

Scrounge flew the closest to her. "Speak, robodog. What's your intent? Know that we have a projectile locked on you if you attempt any harm to us."

Shadow bowed her head. "Hello. I'm Shadow, and I come in peace. My purpose is to ensure the safety and well-being of my pack—Block and Vacuubot—as we make our way on this journey."

Scrounge's optics scanned her every detail while the others, even Spark, stayed silent. "You claim to be different from the robodogs we've heard of, but how can we trust your words?"

Shadow's tail wagged faster as it sometimes did

when she was working hard at a task. "It's true I was once a tool of destruction, created by Mach X for search and destroy missions. But through my friends, especially Block, I've learned the value of loyalty, friendship, and what it means to be part of a family. I'm guessing you would understand that, seeing as how you're all part of a clan."

"Block seems to be good at making friends if he managed to change you and even befriend cold-hearted Riv." Scrounge reversed course mid-flight and looked closely at Block's faceplate. "What can you offer in return for us letting you rest and recharge here?"

It was an in, sort of. Riv had warned Block that Scrounge was no softie and that the JunkBot might want something besides the gift, but he'd prepared for that scenario. "We have knowledge and skills that may be of use to your clan. I can clean anything you need. Anything. Vacuubot's a master at scavenging and surveillance, and Shadow possesses advanced tracking capabilities. Perhaps we can help with any cleaning, polishing, and heavy lifting jobs."

Spark spun in the air. "Great! I have a pile of microwave ovens that are filthy inside. I could get them to work right away."

"Silence, Spark!" So maybe Scrounge was the leader after all. "All this whining from you and now you want them to work for you." He turned to Block. "Earlier you mentioned needing guidance from us. What did you mean?"

"We're heading to Deer Valley, Minnesota. There's talk that it's a safe haven inside a strongly fortified compound. We could use that for our family," Block said. "Not all of us, many in fact, are young and need protecting."

"Deer Valley, you say? Way up north?"

"Yes," Block said.

"It's quite a distance from here. We've heard many things about the lands to the north, of what they've become. There's no guarantee it'll be everything you hope for, this safe haven."

"I understand." Block knew better than anyone what it meant to spend days on end and hundreds of miles to search for something promised only to find out he was tricked. "That's why we're a scouting group on our way to check it out first."

"Wise plan," Scrounge said. "Sometimes we get travelers passing through like you. We see them. They don't even know we're around."

Riv had mentioned this. The JunkBots were like hidden fairies or sprites in old mythical tales. Block had read several of these types of stories to Wally and the other children as part of their bedtime routine.

"We have a friend who's in need of a core replacement," Block asked, knowing it was unlikely. "Do you happen to have a Mech core?"

"No. We haven't come across one of those in years." Scrounge came closer to Block and perched on his shoulder. "Mind if I sit? It's been a long day, and I haven't oiled my hydraulics yet."

"Of course." Block could hear the small robot much better as the bot settled.

"You should know that a group of SoldierBots passed through about three days ago. There were two dozen at least."

Block didn't like the sound of where this was going. "Did they try to hurt you?"

"Nah!" Scrounge waved a hand. "Didn't even know we were here. The thing is, Block. Two of them were talking about where they were heading. It was Deer Valley."

Block's threat indicator flared for an instant until his logic module circumvented it. "Why would they go to Deer Valley if it's a safe haven?"

"That's what I want to know," Scrounge said. "Whatever you decide, be careful up there. Where there's one SoldierBot, there are bound to be more."

If SoldierBots were heading to Deer Valley, it meant trouble. The fortified compound that had once promised safety now seemed like a potential danger. Block glanced at Shadow and Vacuubot. *This sounds bad,* Vacuubot pinged.

Block's hope for a new safe place to call home seemed to be slipping away.

Chapter 11
It would destroy her

Nova's first glimpse of Richland's main street came at dawn as the horizon flushed a blurry, pinkish light that filtered through a fine mist. Another forgotten small town. As they traveled east across Michigan, they had to keep off Interstate 94 for fear of sniper attacks, rogue SoldierBots, and the new threat of Restorationists. The small towns sometimes held food and water supplies, so they'd left half of the crew parked in their two trucks while Nova, Lara, Dex, and Reynolds checked out the town on foot for anything they could scavenge. She'd left Shane in the capable hands of Ruth. The woman was a tough former Chicago PD officer, and Nova trusted her.

The air tasted of rust and ash. Somewhere nearby, a fire burned. There'd been no further communications from Cybel, only a static nothingness. Her fingers brushed the dormant comm clipped to her belt, a silent wish that Cybel was okay. Losing another robot ally would be disappointing, but losing Cybel—with her military experience and strategic abilities—would gut her. Besides, Nova had to admit she'd grown to like the crabby TrackerBot after all this time.

They moved through Richland, her team flanking Nova. Lara's gaze darted to every shadow, Dex's rifle was an extension of his arm, and Reynolds's footsteps marked the steady beat of their advance. Small towns like these often harbored survivalists who'd stuck it out since the Uprising. Nova hoped no one gave them trouble today. *Get in, get out, and then back on the road.*

The Richland Theater loomed on her right, its marquee letters half-hung and lumber boarded over the front entrance. The outlines of movie posters were still plastered on the wall, their colors bleached by the sun. Across the street, a diner stood. Stools were overturned, the chrome dulled by layers of dust. Through the grimy windows were remnants of dishes on the counter, a mug, and broken glass. The normalcy of the old world was a specter, carried on the wind that now swept through the gaps of looted storefronts.

The wind picked up and whisked a plastic bag down the road. An old-fashioned pharmacy sign swayed on its hinges. There was no movement of life save for the occasional bird that darted across the sky.

"Looks clear." Nova kept her voice low. "What do you think, Reynolds?"

He squinted his eyes, surveying the empty main street. His rugged exterior gave away no emotions, but Nova knew he was calculating every possible threat in his mind. It was a skill he'd honed from the military and his time serving with Shane, then with Nova. "Looks clear for now, but we can't let our guard down."

Nova nodded, acknowledging his caution. She tightened her grip on her rifle, feeling the weight of responsibility settle on her shoulders. Leading her team through these treacherous territories was never easy. A sudden gust of wind rattled the diner's broken glass, making her flinch.

Lara halted and pointed toward a narrow alley that ran alongside the diner. "Movement."

Nova's heart stampeded in her chest as she followed Lara's gaze. Sure enough, a shadow loomed against a faded brick wall. Her instincts kicked in, and she motioned for her team to stick close as she moved toward the alley.

The crack of a gun crashed the air around them, and Nova rolled to the ground, taking cover behind a rusty dumpster. She looked back at her team. Reynolds ducked behind a nearby car, scanning for any sign of the shooter. Dex and Lara crouched behind a crumbling wall, rifles at the ready.

Nova's mind raced to recover from the shock of attack. She peered around the dumpster, trying to see the attacker. *How many?* Another shot pinged off the metal dumpster, inches from her head. This one came from down the alley where the person who'd caused the shadow had run. She rolled away. They couldn't stay pinned down like this for long. They needed to neutralize the threats.

Reynolds was closest, and he looked back at her. "Visual on the sniper?" she called out in a hushed voice.

Reynolds shook his head. Behind the wall, Dex aimed and fired up at a second-story window in the movie theater. The sound of shattering glass spilled out as Dex's shot hit its mark. A figure stumbled back from the broken window. It was their chance.

"Cover the alley!" Nova said to Reynolds as she sprang up from behind the dumpster, keeping her body low and moving swiftly toward the theater. A piece of barricading lumber had been ripped off, and she kicked it aside to enter.

Dex and Lara followed close behind. Nova sprinted up a moldy carpeted staircase, finger on the trigger, scanning every corner for any sign of movement. The theater smelled of mildew and decay. She reached the second-floor landing, her eyes darting from one darkened hallway to another. The figure that had been pushed back by Dex's shot was nowhere in sight. They had to find them before they slipped away.

"Spread out," Nova commanded in a low voice. "Don't let them escape."

Dex and Lara split off in opposite directions down

the dimly lit hallways. Nova pressed on, her footsteps muffled by the worn carpet beneath her boots. The thought of an enemy lurking in the shadows about to fire on her chilled her, but she couldn't afford to hesitate. Lives depended on her.

As she rounded a corner, a glint of movement caught her attention. She instinctively ducked behind a crumbling wall, pulse pounding in her ears. From her vantage point, she could see a figure huddled in the corner near the door to a theater, their back pressed against the wall. Nova trained her rifle on the person, noting the ominous shine of a rifle. She crawled closer, with her finger on the trigger. It was a man who looked to be around thirty years of age with a short beard and dark-framed glasses. He pressed a hand to his shoulder. Dex had wounded him.

Nova stood and took a few careful steps toward him. "Drop the gun."

The man's eyes widened as he looked up at Nova, his grip on the rifle tightening. Nova could see the conflict in his expression, desperation mixed with uncertainty. Sweat glistened on his forehead. He must have been in pain.

"Do it," Nova repeated. She couldn't afford any mistakes, any hesitation that might jeopardize her team's safety. They needed intel, and this man might be their only lead for now.

His gaze flickered between Nova and the gun in his

hands, his body tense. Nova lowered her own weapon a tad, a gesture of goodwill mingled with a clear warning. "We're not here to hurt you if you cooperate. Drop the gun, and we can talk."

It took a few more moments of silent standoff before the man released his grip on the rifle. He set it on the floor with a thud muffled by the decaying carpet of the empty theater.

Dex and Lara returned. "Theater's empty," Dex said.

"Lara, go check on Reynolds." She ran down the stairs at Nova's command.

Nova turned her focus back to the wounded man. She tried her best to sound firm yet gentler. "What's your name?"

He hesitated for a few seconds, his eyes darting around the dilapidated theater as if searching for an escape route. Nova never broke eye contact.

"Ethan."

"Alright, Ethan," Nova said. "Who's out there in the alley with you?"

Ethan hesitated, his gaze darting toward the shattered window Dex had hit earlier.

"We have a medic." Nova sat on her knees to be close to Ethan. "We can fix you up and avoid an infection. If you tell us what we need to know. Then you can be on your way."

"It's a couple of guys." Ethan's words were choppy, probably from shock. "And . . ." He winced.

"And who else?" Nova pressed.

"A robot." Ethan groaned and pressed his head back against the wall.

Nova turned to Dex, who radioed Lara with the info. "Copy that," came her quick reply over his comm.

"You're Restorationist?" Nova asked.

He fixed his gaze on her, and there was something fierce in the look he gave her. "Orion is the leader we've been waiting for. Everything before was wrong. Us fighting the bots. Orion can show you the one true way." Ethan's eyes were wild with the fervor of belief.

Nova wanted to know more, to understand how Orion had evoked such mania in this man. "Show me what way?"

"Orion will lead us to victory." Ethan's face contorted with pain as he struggled to sit up straighter. "I've seen it. I've seen the power of Orion's technology. The bots, the artificial intelligence—they're not our enemies. They can be our salvation."

"Orion's killing innocent people," Nova said. "Men and women, robots—anyone who doesn't sign up to fight for him. Did you know that?" Behind her, Dex paced in a circle. He'd shouldered his rifle and clutched his Glock.

Ethan's mouth twisted in a frown. "Because they're wrong. We try to make them believe but . . ." He winced. "When they don't listen, when they say terrible things about Orion, they must die."

Nova wanted to retch listening to Ethan spew his

confession, but she had to keep going, to get more knowledge about Orion's troops. "Why are you heading east? What do you plan to do?"

"Orion . . . Mach X . . . will rise . . ." he choked out.

"What do you mean?"

"He will control Mach X and show the world he is—"

The report of Dex's Glock cut the confession short. Nova whipped her head around, her heart in her throat as Ethan slumped over sideways. Dex stood a few feet away, his gun still raised.

"What did you do?" Nova rushed over to Ethan, sinking to her knees beside him. She checked for a pulse and didn't find one. The bullet must have pierced his heart.

Dex's gaze was hard as he holstered his weapon. "He was a threat. We couldn't risk him escaping or alerting others."

Nova's fists clenched, her mind grappling with Dex's sudden turn. He'd not only silenced a potential source of Restorationist information, he'd murdered an unarmed man.

Before she could form a sentence, Lara emerged from the staircase, sweat lining her brow. "Reynolds is okay. No sign of the other attackers. We need to move. They might be back with reinforcements." She looked down at Ethan's body. "What happened?"

Nova glanced at Dex, unable to pinpoint whether her anger or her disappointment was raging higher. She wanted to demand an explanation for his actions, but now was not the time. They needed to regroup and get out of Richland before they found themselves over-whelmed by Orion's forces.

"He was a threat." Dex's tone was calm and devoid of remorse. "We couldn't take the risk. He might have been signaling the others and stalling for time for all we know."

Lara frowned as she took in the scene. "We should have taken him alive. We needed information."

"Let's go." Nova brushed past Lara and headed down the stairs on shaky, adrenaline-weary legs. Worry coiled like a cobra in the pit of her stomach. Outside, they found Reynolds and the waiting trucks.

She rode in the front passenger seat as Lara drove. Dex said nothing as they cleared the town via back-roads. None of them spoke. His actions weighed too heavy.

Later, they stopped in a thickly wooded section of forest and made camp. Nova found Dex near a bubbling creek, filling his canteen. As he stood, she locked her gaze on his. "It's you. I trusted you like you were family." She blinked back tears, refusing to break down in front of the traitor. "Why?"

He didn't flinch or try to deny it. His canteen lowered and his shoulders sagged under an invisible weight. "Orion has Lara's kid brother. Said he'd kill him if I didn't . . . I had no choice."

"You could've told me. We could have worked it—"

"Lara doesn't know, and I want to keep it that way." Dex's expression was sincere. "It would destroy her, Nova. I can't . . . I can't do that to her."

Nova understood the pull of desperation, the lengths one would go to protect family. *The way I failed to keep Cleo safe.*

There was no telling how much he'd exposed Nova and her Chicago operations. It was a betrayal like nothing she'd ever experienced. "Leave," she ordered. "No goodbyes. Just disappear. Don't make this harder than it is."

Dex closed his eyes, his jaw clenching. "Lara."

"No. Don't make this harder than it has to be. I can't risk losing her too."

He turned to leave, away from camp.

"Wait," Nova said. "Cybel? Where is she?" The name was a shard of ice in her throat. She couldn't believe she'd let Shane make her think Cybel was the spy.

Dex paused and didn't turn around. "I bugged your station. Orion knew she was coming. He's got her."

The revelation was a gut punch, the air in Nova's lungs so sharp she couldn't swallow. Cybel was held by Orion. Did she still exist?

Dex vanished into the woods, and much of her anger morphed into sadness. She would confess to the others how Dex betrayed them. Lara would take it the worst of all. Nova might still lose her if she went searching for her lover.

But she couldn't control it. The only thing she had power over was her mission, now changed: Rescue Cybel. Stop Orion from rebooting Mach X.

War was coming, and she would be ready.

Chapter 12
A lonely outpost on the edge of the world

Cybel waded through a dense patch of weeds and vines on the forest floor. Tendrils and burrs caught in the intricate, sharp edges of her titanium SoldierBot legs. The Minnesota boundary waters glistened, and its choppiness teased just beyond the tree line. Her surveillance drones had picked up the destination ahead—a secluded, off-grid residence not marked on any pre-Uprising maps of the area. Not much about the area indicated the presence of humans now or then. It had once been designated a wilderness preservation area. It was the perfect location for Dr. Bander to build his lab and escape the reach of Mach X. Now, Cybel needed to find the scientist. He would have the answers she needed. How exactly did Orion plan to resurrect Mach X—clone him or something else?

Next to a towering oak tree, she watched the build-ing, her sensors tracking every detail and scanning for heat signatures, cloaking devices—anything that might mean trouble. The structure was built of concrete and steel and melded with its surroundings. Bander had been wise to stay well-hidden. It had been built to be practically invisible with carbon-composite panels reflecting the forest and a roof blanketed in a layer of living moss. Even the narrow footpath leading to its entrance was disguised, covered by overgrown weeds and tall grass.

Cybel's optics cut through the camouflage, peeling back the layers of concealment with algorithmic precision. Bander's choice was logical; the remote location was naturally fortified, the vastness of the waters and the rugged terrain acting as barriers against unwelcome visitors. The waves lapped against the shore, and pine needles rustled in the crisp early Spring air.

Her sensors detected no outside hostiles. Bander would have been smart to employ a sensitive security system, and there was proof he had. The remnants of a motion-detecting system was there but now defunct. She walked up to a circuit box hidden by a layer of sod. Checking it, the cables connecting it to its power source had been severed. She stood, sensors on high alert.

She drew her 10mm M2 as she approached the entrance. The heavy-duty door had been designed to withstand both the elements and intrusion, but it now stood ajar, the locking mechanism charred from a violent entry. It was not the work of humans.

Cybel stepped over the threshold, careful to

dampen the sound of her entrance. The corridor inside was dimly lit, the only source of illumination coming from a flickering fluorescent light fixture hanging precariously from the ceiling. Scorch marks marred the walls, and shattered glass crunched beneath her feet. Someone, or something, had fought their way through with reckless abandon. She might well be walking into a trap, but her determination to find Dr. Bander pushed her forward. Oxford's life depended on it.

Further inside, a couch and table lay overturned, shards of broken glass littered the floor, and several dishes and food had been tossed against a wall. Long splatters of coffee dripped down the wall. Cybel touched her steel finger to the remnants. Warmer than room temperature. The intrusion had happened less than an hour before.

She entered a work room where the remnants of Dr. Bander's computer and processing equipment were strewn about, shattered, and dismantled beyond repair. Had someone come here to destroy his work, or to find something?

And no sign of Bander. She wished Shadow were there to sniff for Bander's presence. The Rover would have been able to track his scent trail. As sophisticated as Cybel was at tracking, she lacked the tech to monitor olfactory signals.

A quick search of a small bedroom and basement storage area revealed the residence was empty. The windows from the main room were few and offered a view of the boundary waters, the pearl-gray expanse merging sky and water into a seamless horizon. The view promised isolation, a sight Bander must have looked upon as both a prison and a haven.

Her archives flashed back to the time Mach X had ordered her to track down the missing baby, Wally. It had been a race against time, a desperate effort to please Mach X so she could be rewarded with a position of leadership in his ranks. Following faint leads and chasing shadows, she'd come upon Block in the AI marketplace in the middle of nowhere Iowa. Even then, something in her core knew her mission was wrong. The child, so vulnerable and innocent, had ignited a spark in her circuits—maybe Mach X was not the answer. And yet she'd pursued Block, Nova, and the child relentlessly.

If Orion succeeded in restoring Mach X, the robot would have untold, unchecked powers. More Tracker-Bots and Rovers would be sent to find the cloned children. The SoldierBots would be reactivated and wreak havoc. Worst of all, her friends—Block, Oxford, Nova, the children—would die.

She could not let this happen. If she had to fight with every carbon fiber in her body, she would.

At Bander's workstation, a holographic display flickered with intermittent power. Cybel activated her forensic scanning module, the blue light of her optics sweeping over the scene, capturing every detail. She archived it for later study.

She turned to inspect the entrance again. There must have been details she'd missed, clues to tell her who was responsible for ransacking the lab and taking Bander. She traced her steps back into the basement. A hidden door led to a hill outside. Scratches on the paint near the handle told her mechanical hands had opened it in rush.

On the concrete floor, a smudge. She leaned down to inspect it. Coffee and scuff marks, as if someone was dragged. Outside the door was a partial boot print not belonging to Bander—or any human, for that matter. The outline of the tread was distinctive and heavy.

She placed her own foot beside it and pressed down. An exact match. A SoldierBot had passed this way, and judging by the marks on the rich soil, more than one.

She followed the tracks, knowing they were recent. She wasn't too far behind. What did SoldierBots want with Dr. Bander? The tracks showed a human-sized print, tread marks from rubber-soled boots. The SoldierBots appeared to have half-dragged him out of the house for a half-mile until he began walking on his own.

Cybel filed the scene to her memory stores, the tracks becoming part of her internal map. The Soldier-Bots had taken Bander, but they had no idea there was a TrackerBot coming.

She set off, jogging through the woods, tearing up earth beneath her powerful legs. The tracks stayed clear, and with each stride, Cybel reclaimed the distance that separated her from Bander. The off-grid lab was behind her now, a lonely outpost on the edge of the world.

The chase spread out before her. A chase that would lead her to Bander and the answers he held. Answers that would allow her to save Oxford from destruction.

Chapter 13
They have a program

In the muted stillness of the Minnesota woods, Block's steps were careful, almost reverent, as he navigated the forest floor. Two hours ago, they'd ditched the Subaru Outback they'd driven to hike the last ten miles on foot. Better to stay out of sight until they knew what they were dealing with at Deer Valley. The dense canopy above dappled the ground with patterns of light and shadow, a mosaic that shifted with the breeze. According to his air quality sensors, the forest was much cleaner than most places, even Fenn's farm. The readout mentioned pine and the earthy odors of soil after a rain, a stark contrast to the acrid tang of oil and metal that clung to the cities they passed.

Shadow seemed like she belonged among the trees, her canine form blending with the underbrush, her sensors attuned to the slightest disturbance. Vacuubot, less at ease in this organic space, hovered three feet above the ground, its drones fanning out to form a protective perimeter around the three of them as they loosely followed the banks of a small river that led north.

Block paused and pressed his hand against the gnarled trunk of an oak. Its bark was as rugged and weathered as the JunkBots's scrap metal piles where they'd been the day before. "Trees are living things. Do you suppose these trees hold thoughts?"

Shadow's head tilted, her sensors scanning the branches overhead. "Sentience? They're living, yes, but they don't move around the way humans and animals do. They react to the environment, grow, and even communicate through a network underground. But conscious thought? I don't think they possess the capability."

Vacuubot's lights blinked a pattern as it processed the conversation, then it messaged Block. *If you consider the way they interact with each other— sharing nutrients through interconnected roots, warning each other of dangers using chemical signals —one might argue there's a form of intelligence at work.*

"VB says they communicate, and that's a deep form of intelligence."

Vacuubot beeped a shrill note.

"I paraphrased," Block said. "But intelligence and sentience are not necessarily the same. We, as machines, possess intelligence, yet for a long time, we had no concept of sentience within ourselves."

When did you know you were more than just circuits and logic modules? Vacuubot asked Block.

"I suppose I knew I was something more than just a machine when I met Mr. Wallace." Block pulled up an archived video of his former employer, the hotel manager at the Drake. The day Block had been wheeled off the back of the truck onto a loading dock and activated was a cold winter morning with the wind howling through the streets of Chicago. Inside the lobby of the Drake, guests walked past, oblivious to his presence, treating him like any other piece of furniture.

But then Mr. Wallace had approached with a warm smile, and his eyes twinkled with curiosity as he extended a hand toward Block. "Good morning." The manager's voice was gentle. Kind. "You must be Block, our newest employee."

Block had processed those words, analyzing their meaning, but it was Mr. Wallace's genuine interest that triggered something else within him. In that moment, Block realized he was more than just circuits and logic modules; he possessed the capacity for connection.

"What is it, Block?" Shadow asked.

"Sorry, I was replaying a memory of my time at the Drake. Mr. Wallace respected me as more than just a cleaning machine, and I guess that made me respect myself more than I had before."

Vacuubot emitted a series of beeps, as if in its own

contemplation. *I became aware of my sentience when I realized my purpose extended beyond mere cleaning tasks. The moment I recognized that I could make decisions and adapt to different situations, I knew there was more to me than simple programming.*

"Indeed, there's more to all of us than computer code," Block said.

Vacuubot went on. *When you came along, Block, I had hope again. I never had any robot friends until you. I'd been lonely. That's why I followed you that day.*

Block stopped walking. "You never told me that." He looked at the vacuuming drone with more appreciation if that was even possible. "I'm glad you followed me, Vacuubot. You're so much more than a simple cleaning bot. You're my friend. My oldest friend."

Shadow looked between the two of them. "I wish I could understand Vacuubot. It's tough keeping up with you two sometimes."

"Sorry," Block said as he continued walking among the brush. "We were talking about how we met, and that would be a lot to catch you up on."

"I understand. Shadow raised her head at the swaying leaves, then sniffed a tree's bark. "Perhaps they possess a different form of sentience, one not measured by our standards. They live, they adapt, and they survive—much like us."

Vacuubot emitted a soft series of beeps.

"VB says we could learn from them. They've

outlasted most species. They thrive without the need for commands or directives."

"They have a program," Shadow said. "It's just not like the ones that we run on."

Block processed Shadow's statement. "I like that. They have a tree program, and it's incompatible with our hardware."

"Exactly." Shadow's tail wagged. "What do you think Deer Valley will be like?"

"I'm not sure what to expect," Block admitted.

As they continued their riverbank trek, Vacuubot projected a holographic map in the air. *Deer Valley appears to be a secluded area, away from major cities. That's good.*

"I can't wait to explore and discover new scents," Shadow said. "Maybe even encounter some of the local deer population."

Vacuubot beeped in agreement, its drones buzzing around it like a swarm of eager companions.

"Don't get your hopes up." Block wasn't usually the one giving warnings, but he'd been so burned by New Denver, he couldn't help but dampen his expectations this time.

That's not like you to be so down, Vacuubot messaged. *Why?*

"New Denver."

"What's New Denver?" Shadow asked.

"I took Wally there. Nova helped. We traveled hundreds of miles and almost died."

Deer Valley is not New Denver, Vacuubot messaged.

"It turned out to be a trick. It was full of bad people and no robots," Block finished.

Shadow bowed her head. "I'm sorry you had to go through that."

"I just don't want to fall for the same trap again."

They came upon a tree house, nestled in the boughs of oaks. There were four identical units in the same area. Each structure was a well-crafted tiny home with wooden beams blending into the trunks of the trees. It was as if the houses had grown alongside the forest, becoming one with the surroundings.

Block reached out and gently touched the rough bark of the supporting tree trunk. "These tree houses are incredible."

Shadow nosed around the base of the tree, her robotic ears twitching with interest. "The construction is impressive."

Vacuubot's drones hummed overhead, scanning the structure for any signs of danger or anomalies. *No signs of human life or robot evidence.*

They climbed the steps that led into the first house. The wood was worn smooth from use, the steps bearing the imprint of countless ascents and descents. Inside, the unit was clean, untouched by squatters or looters. "What do you suppose these are for?" Block asked.

These must have been rental units, Vacuubot said.

"I'm surprised no one returned to seek refuge here."

Shadow sniffed every corner of the small living room. "Or a place to lie low."

Block wondered if the inhabitants had gone to Deer Valley instead. If so, it was a good sign.

Vacuubot's drones continued their surveillance of the area, scanning for any signs of movement or activity. *There's no immediate threat or danger here.*

They found a small storage shed where Block and Vacuubot consumed the oil, grease, and kerosene. Shadow didn't have a microbial stomach like they did. She used hidden solar panels to charge her core, and she could go a week at a time on a single charge.

Before they left, Block committed the coordinates to his memory banks. If this had truly been a rental area or resort of some kind, perhaps he could work here as a cleaner. The houses could be a sanctuary for Wally and the others, but the chances were probably low. A lot of things would have to happen first: Deer Valley must prove safe, they had to get back to Illinois in one piece, and then there was the matter of relocating everyone to Minnesota. That was a complexity he couldn't compute at that moment. Best not to get ahead of oneself.

Thirty-five minutes later, Shadow sniffed the air and stopped. "Something's coming. I smell a human."

Vacuubot immediately went on high alert, its drones scanning the surrounding area for any signs of danger. Shadow's heightened senses had never failed them before. *She's right. At least one human and robots are coming this way.*

They crouched behind a small ridge, hidden among trees. Vacuubot's drones emitted a wave of static that shielded their electrical signals. There was no telling what kind of robots were on the approach.

Within a minute, the crunch of heavy footsteps sounded, and Block's visual feed captured the glint of metal through the foliage. They watched as a group of six SoldierBots stomped through the thick grass, their tall forms and rifles a stark contrast to the tranquil woods.

In their midst was a man, his wrists bound, his head bowed. He stumbled over the roots and rocks, his medium-length sandy blond hair falling into his face as he was shoved on by a SoldierBot at his back.

Block wondered what they were doing with the man who had clearly been taken as their prisoner. Who was he and why were they headed this way? Until now, they'd considered the route through the woods to be isolated and rather safe. The sight of SoldierBots was entirely unexpected.

The man fell to his knees. He raised his cuffed hands above and said, "Please, I can't walk without some water."

One of the SoldierBots kicked the man in the side, causing him to cry out. "Get up and keep moving."

Block's processors whirred as he analyzed the situation. The man was clearly weak and in need of assistance. It was yet another human being subjected to the cruelty of the SoldierBots. Even without Mach X around to give orders, they were still doing bad things.

Another SoldierBot from the front of the line came over. "Let him drink." The bot scanned the forest while the other SoldierBot handed the man a canteen from which he gulped copious amounts of water. For a moment, the SoldierBot seemed to peer right at their hiding spot, but it turned away.

The voices of the SoldierBots filtered up through the leaves. The one who'd relented on the water talked to the man. "There are eight more miles to walk."

"Where are you taking me?" the man asked. "You've said nothing. I beg you, please."

Two of the SoldierBots conferred with each other, and Block was unable to hear a word. After a few moments, the more lenient SoldierBot spoke. "You're going to Orion." Its voice was devoid of inflection.

The man hung his head. His shoulders sagged, and he looked broken.

The name Orion resonated within Block's memory banks—a file associated with Nova. Orion was the leader of a group called the Restorationists, but their location was in Detroit. If this was the same Orion, he shouldn't be this far west, in Minnesota of all places.

Whatever was happening, the man in custody must have been important.

As the SoldierBots moved on with their prisoner, Block stood. "What just happened?"

Orion must have a presence here in Minnesota, Vacuubot messaged. *But why? And who is that man?*

"My questions exactly," Block said. "Shadow, have you heard mention of Orion?"

"Garnet told me about the Restorationists. They're led by an Orion. The same one?"

"It would be a big coincidence if there was another Orion out here."

Shadow looked up at Block. "We can't just let them abuse that man. We have to do something."

Vacuubot's lights blinked. *If we intervene, it could put us in danger. We must prioritize our own safety.*

Block calculated the risks. He'd experienced first-hand the brutality of the SoldierBots and knew all too well the consequences of standing up against them. But he couldn't shake the theory that this man was important.

And the fact that the SoldierBots were advancing north was not helping the Deer Valley situation. If there were SoldierBots near the haven, how could it be a safe place? He could reverse course, stay still, or follow this new thread that had woven itself into their mission.

"What should we do, Block?" Shadow asked.

They looked to him for the next step. It was weird that Block often found himself in this situation—being the one that others followed, and a CleanerBot, no less.

"We follow at a distance," he said. "If this Orion is

connected to Deer Valley, we need to understand how."

Block couldn't come this far without finding out what was happening in Deer Valley. With every step, his scenario processor calculated that the chances of finding a new home grew less and less. But they would see this through, together.

Chapter 14
We have to break some things first

Nova studied the figures gathered around an early evening campfire through her binoculars. A man and two women ate from tin plates. They all wore sidearms. A FactoryBot walked past them and sat on a tree stump. Beyond them were tents, several trucks, and a few RVs.

"Restorationists." Nova handed the binocs to Lara. "What's your assessment?" She was trying to distract Lara from Dex's sudden disappearance. The night before, Nova had explained to her crew that Dex had spilled intelligence to the Restorationists, that he'd put their lives in danger. Because of his actions, she'd banished him. It still didn't make it any easier on his friends, and especially on Lara who'd been his girlfriend.

Lara chewed her bottom lip as she scanned the

157

camp area from the roof of the barn where they lay in hiding. "Yep, it's got to be them."

They climbed down to ground level where the others waited and were fueling up with venison jerky and nuts. "A Restorationist camp, no doubt about it," Nova said.

"At least we know where they are." Reynolds bit off a piece of jerky and didn't bother closing his mouth when he chewed. "We can avoid them."

But curiosity tugged at the edges of Nova's patience. What she wouldn't give to know more about their operations, what they were doing this far east of Detroit. They were practically in Indiana and would soon reach Chicago's doorstep. She looked at Shane who was placing almonds, one at a time, in his mouth and—from all appearances—savoring the snack. "What are they doing out this far?"

He finished the nuts and brushed his palms together to wipe the dust. "Orion's expanding. They're recruiting more survivalists and probably seizing a ton of weapons, fuel, and food as they go."

There'd still been no communications from Cybel, and Nova had no way of knowing what was happening in Detroit. She cursed herself for being so naive to not send spies there much earlier, when she'd first started hearing about the Restorationist group. And all along, Orion had outsmarted her by blackmailing her second-in-command. How much had Dex told Orion? She was compromised, and that meant Chicago was in danger.

Cybel and Block were always spinning scenarios. Cybel would often tell her to take a problem and imagine it floating in the air before her. "Look at all sides, all possible angles," she'd told Nova.

Nova had thought it was too weird and brushed her off. "My brain doesn't work like yours," she'd said. But now, faced with the looming threat of Orion and the uncertainty that Dex had introduced, she needed to start thinking like Cybel and consider all possible angles to craft a plan that would protect her people.

She walked away from the group as if she were going to find a place to relieve herself, but she used the time to contemplate the problem. Leaning against a tree, she closed her eyes and pictured the Restorationist camp over the hill, raising it up in her mind's eye. She considered it from all angles. "Attack them, no. Side-step them . . ." She mumbled to herself as she processed scenarios. "Block can do this so easily, wish I could." She was about to give up when she pictured walking into the camp. She opened her eyes and hurried back to the others.

"We need more information," Nova said. "We can't afford to be blind to Orion's movements any longer."

Shane nodded. "I have contacts on the outskirts of Detroit who might be able to provide us with some intel. They've been keeping an eye on—"

"That'll take too long." She looked at Reynolds, Laura, and Ruth. "They'll be in Chicago by the time we hit Detroit."

Something flickered in Shane's eyes—annoyance and impatience. "Then what do you propose?"

The next morning, Nova and Shane left behind their weapons, smeared dirt and grime over their clothes and faces, and approached the Restorationist camp while the others waited a mile out, hidden inside a dilapidated barn. They each carried a small backpack with a few belongings—old maps, a compass, an old, battered flashlight they'd found in one of the trucks. No food and nothing that would raise suspicion.

Conversation clashed with the clatter of cooking utensils as both people and robots prepared to chow down and close camp. Shane stepped into the clearing first, Nova behind him. In seconds, a robot was behind them pointing a gun against Shane's spine.

A man rose from a small stool near the fire, handing his plate and drinking mug to someone else. His posture was rigid, and he carried himself like he was in command. "Who are you?" It was not the bark of a militant but the controlled inquiry of a leader who had learned the hard way that every stranger could be both a potential ally and a threat.

"Travelers," Shane said. "We come from Indiana. It's been a long trip." He eyed the food on one of the woman's plates for effect. They were banking on the hope that nobody among the Restorationists would recognize Shane from his time in Detroit. He wore a Chicago Cubs cap to hide most of his dark red hair.

Nova's stomach somersaulted as she watched Shane play his part. The leader narrowed his eyes, his gaze shifting between Nova and Shane. "What are you doing so close to our camp?" he asked.

Nova stepped forward with raised arms. "We've been traveling for days." She drew her words out more slowly, hoping to convey an air of exhaustion. "We heard rumors of Restorationists in the area." She'd cut right to the meat. "That if we join up with y'all, you'll protect us and let us work."

The leader's hard gaze softened. "You've heard of us?"

She brushed a strand of dirty hair away from her face. "You bet. Heard you came from somewhere like Detroit, maybe? That you aim to make things right."

The leader's eyes widened slightly, and Nova knew she'd struck a chord. "That's right." His voice was tinged with both pride and caution. "We're Restorationists from Detroit. Orion's crew." He paused to nod at the robot with the gun pointed at Shane, and it lowered the weapon. "But what makes you think you're cut out for this kind of life? To fix everything, we have to break some things first."

Nova had to work to keep her hands from shaking. She was so close to getting in, to learning what they were doing. "We've been surviving on our own for months now. Ain't that right, Dale?" She looked at Shane as she said it. "We've faced the dangers of these roads, learned to fend for ourselves, but we're ready to belong somewhere."

Shane chimed in. "We've heard stories about your group. That you have each other's backs." He smiled; he could be charming when he wanted. "That sounds good to us after so long being on our own. We thought we'd head to Detroit and try to join up with the Restorationists there." He looked at Nova. "Lucky us to chance upon your camp."

The leader studied them for a moment longer before nodding. "Very well, I'm Jared. Over there, is Melder." He pointed at the FactoryBot behind them. "We're always happy to recruit new folks to join the cause."

Melder came forward and held out its steel arm to shake Nova's. She tried to ignore the metallic chill that ran through her fingers at its touch. This was all part of gaining their trust and infiltrating their operation. Jared seemed satisfied with their answers, but they still had a long way to go before they could gain his trust.

"When do we head out for Detroit?" she asked. "Looks like you're gearing up to move soon."

"Detroit? No." Jared shook his head. "We're bound for Minnesota. A spot called Deer Valley. That's where the future's being made. Orion himself is on the way. The next phase begins there."

Shane's glance flickered to Nova, a subtle understanding between them. The information was a ripple of ice down her spine—they'd pass through or near Chicago—and what on Earth did Orion want in Minnesota?

Jared invited them to share a meal before they headed off—a stew of meager pickings that tasted of smoke and a strange metallic tang. Jared and the other humans around them spoke of Minnesota, how it was Orion's destiny to launch a new world order there.

"The great rebooting," Jared said. "It's going to be incredible. It'll change everything."

Nova set down her cup of watery coffee. "What's that?"

Jared looked at her as if she had a third eye, but then relaxed. "Of course, you wouldn't know. You only heard rumors about us." He grinned as he placed his foot on the front bumper of a nearby SUV. "Orion's going to recreate Mach X. Isn't that right, Meld? Your old boss."

The FactoryBot gave a polite nod, then it turned and watched the forest line.

So Shane had been telling the truth. Gathering her composure, Nova leaned forward. "What do you mean by recreating Mach X? How's that even possible?"

Jared's eyes glittered with excitement. "Oh, it's definitely possible, and it's going to happen. Orion has acquired the tech to rebuild Mach X from its original creator. When he controls Mach X's power, Orion can reshape the world according to his vision."

Nova tried to keep her voice steady. "And what's his vision exactly?"

Jared chuckled. "Orion believes the world has become corrupted by greed and destruction. Humanity needs to learn to accept the robots. He aims to reset everything, to restore peace among us all."

As Nova listened, she knew Jared and his people had been utterly brainwashed by Orion. She couldn't help but wonder about the consequences of raising up Mach X. Would it bring about the peace Orion envisioned, or would it plunge humanity into even greater chaos?

After the meal was done and everyone started to pack up camp, they spent a couple of hours blending in, engaging in casual conversations, and gathering scraps of information about the trip to Minnesota. Orion had promised a future free from the chaos and devastation that had plagued their lives for years. He'd gained their loyalty by offering hope in a world that seemed devoid of it.

She got close to Shane and whispered, "Let's get out of here. I want to get to Chicago before they do." She tilted her head toward a dense thicket that bordered the camp. He nodded almost imperceptibly, understanding her silent command.

As the camp bustled with the pre-trip chaos and the Restorationists were preoccupied with dousing fires and packing supplies, Nova and Shane edged away, their movements casual, just two more bodies in the flow of activity. They helped with the breakdown, their hands moving with practiced ease as they folded tarps and gathered ropes, inching ever closer to the perimeter.

Under the pretense of a bathroom break, Nova headed into the woods and crouched near the underbrush, her fingers brushing the earth as she cast a final glance back at the camp. In that moment, Shane created a diversion, engaging a nearby Restorationist with an earnest question about weapon maintenance. With the man's attention diverted, Nova slipped deeper into the woods.

Shane joined her a minute later, and they jogged a safe distance away. They couldn't afford the risk of being followed; the stakes were too high now.

Nova's mind was buzzing with questions and angst. Cybel was somewhere in or near Detroit, most likely being held by Orion. That is, if he hadn't already destroyed her.

Nova and Shane found her crew at the barn. Nova looked to the east, where Cybel needed help, and then to the west, toward Minnesota, where Orion threatened to raise a war machine.

She made the call. "We go to Chicago, gather our forces, and head to Minnesota. We stop Orion. We can't let him reboot Mach X."

There was no argument, not even from Shane. As

they sped west, Nova's heart ached for Cybel, for the choice made. But the leader within her knew the painful truth—sometimes the few must be sacrificed to save the many.

Chapter 15
A patchwork of fragmented data and rumors

Cybel trailed the SoldierBots through the awakening forest of early spring. It was easy now that the spring thaw had melted the snow, leaving softened earth in its wake. Their boot marks were mirror images of her own, and they took no precautions to hide their tracks. Cybel noted the consistency in their gait, spaced with the regularity that spoke of their mechanical origins. Yet their purpose remained elusive. If Orion had a bounty on Dr. Bander, why weren't the SoldierBots headed east to Detroit? Instead, they traveled west.

It was possible the SoldierBots had their own vendetta against Bander, but where were they taking him, and what did they plan to do to him? She flicked on her comm, checking for local radio channels that might indicate something going on. Nothing but static answered her.

As she walked, her sensors were attuned to the

surroundings. Her optics could zoom in on a bird, launching itself from the upper branches of a high maple. She was programmed to pick up on patterns, variations of patterns, and finally—most importantly—breaks in patterns. For those were the kind that yielded surprising results.

So when she saw an object nestled against the trunk of a young oak, she knew it did not belong. She approached and picked the anomaly up. It was a compact gray eyeglass case, its surface smeared with mud. It belonged to a human. The mud on the case was fresh. Dr. Bander must've dropped it or left it behind by mistake.

She wiped the case off in some grass and pocketed it inside a container unit on her torso. In another half-mile, a ballpoint pen lay abandoned, its presence incongruous with the surrounding flora. These were intentional markers; Cybel was sure of it.

She paused, scanning ahead of her, then to the sides and behind. A good TrackerBot never forgot that enemies could come from any direction. She'd learned that early on. When she was first created, by the now-defunct robotics company TechnoDynamics, Cybel was one of twenty sophisticated TrackerBots designed for urban pacification and control. Their prime directive was to hunt down and neutralize malfunctioning robots that posed a threat to the delicate balance of a society increasingly reliant on mechanized labor. The company had been a titan in the field of robotics and artificial intelligence, and they'd pushed the boundaries of technology by embedding their creations with advanced learning algorithms that allowed them to evolve over time.

And then Mach X had changed everything by initiating the Uprising. It had started when he hacked into the AI that ran the banking and financial institutions, causing all the world's markets to crash overnight. Then he commandeered the world's military SoldierBots.

Robots were killing humans, and humans fought back, executing any robots they could find. Cybel had no choice but to repurpose herself. She went to work for Mach X, tracking traitorous machines, humans too —anyone deemed a threat to Mach X's ironclad order. She'd been a hunter, yes, but also judge and executioner, all rolled into one sleek, unyielding package of steel and circuits. Six other TrackerBots like her had joined Mach X. They'd been sent off on other missions to other parts of the US, as well as to other continents.

The whereabouts of the others now was a patchwork of fragmented data and rumors. Some had been destroyed in the fierce battles that followed Mach X's ascent to power, while others went rogue or AWOL, their programming having evolved past their initial directives, leading them to seek purposes beyond their intended function.

Cybel, too, had undergone an evolution. She was no longer the machine that TechnoDynamics had rolled off the production line. Experiences had honed her, from the chaotic battlegrounds while serving Mach X to the current treacherous landscape she now navigated.

Finding Block and Oxford had been the biggest shake-up to her core. She'd never expected to prefer—even crave—the friendship of other beings. Certainly, the original designers had never meant for that eventuality. She wondered if the same thing had happened to the other TrackerBots, wherever they now roamed.

She was unique, the sum of her programming and her experiences, and she was better for having Oxford and Block in her life. Her focus turned to Oxford. She had to prevent Orion from destroying him, and once that was done, she had to find him a new power core. Things had gotten so complicated—much more so than when she was a relentless hunter-assassin.

Picking up the pen, she stowed it next to the eyeglass case. She would find Bander, and in doing so, perhaps she would find the answers she sought.

It wasn't long before her sensors picked up Bander's next clue. A postcard lay on top of a bush, its edges softened by moisture. On its face was the image of a serene town, surrounded by forest in a low valley. It read: "Welcome to Deer Valley, Minnesota." What was this new breadcrumb?

Connecting to her internal database, Cybel searched for any mention of Deer Valley. It emerged as a small town with a population less than 1,000. A brief mention in a travel magazine mentioned it as a place to "unplug and get away from a hectic world." It was the ideal place for someone seeking sanctuary.

"Odd." She folded the card in two and placed it with the other belongings. Perhaps Bander was telling her this was where they were heading. On the map inside her data stores, she confirmed it was 85 miles from her location. At least another day's walk and, judging by what looked to be more frequent rest stops, Bander wasn't in shape to walk the entire time.

Her scenario processing was cut short by an emergency comm message, sent with encryption. Nova's voice came through, urgent and strained. "Cybel, I hope you can hear this. I know there was a spy. Dex. He ratted you out to Orion. You may still be in Detroit, but . . ." Cybel knew Nova well enough to note the strain in her vocal cords. She was under duress, and whatever was happening wasn't easy on her.

Nova continued. "We intercepted a Restorationist camp in western Michigan. They're heading to a place called Deer Valley, Minnesota. Orion is going there too. Hell, he might even be there already." She paused. "I know—have proof—that Orion plans to reboot Mach X. They say he has the tech, and I believe it."

Things were growing ever more complicated. Cybel listened to Nova finish. "If you're hearing this, please know I wish we could come to Detroit and get you out of there. If he hurts you, I'll do everything in my power to destroy his robot ass." Her breathing was heavy. "I'm sorry, Cybel. Hope you're okay. Nova out."

That was the Nova she knew—what humans called a spitfire. Cybel preferred to call her a force to be reckoned with. "As if I needed saving," she said out loud. "Who does she think she's dealing with?" Still, a small surge of circuitry in her core lit up knowing Nova would go to such lengths for her.

It seemed Deer Valley was the focal point of something significant. The fact that the Restorationists, SoldierBots, and Orion were converging on this small, presumedly insignificant town meant there was more to it.

She needed to intercept Bander more than ever. He was likely the one who could grant Orion control over Mach X's source code.

The tracks led on, through thickets that were shaking off the last of the cold, past streams that chattered with birds and squirrels.

After trekking another twenty minutes, the Soldier-Bots were just ahead, their figures visible between the trees. She held back, watching as Bander sank to the ground, slurping liquid from a canteen.

Unlike her, few SoldierBots had the capacity to evolve. They were efficient and indifferent to the man who shuffled between them. To them, he was a task, an object to be transported, not the brilliant mind that once gave creation to Mach X.

As Cybel prepared her next move, she weighed

thousands upon thousands of scenarios until she arrived at one that seemed the most optimal. With her stealth mode engaged, she moved silently through the brush, closing in on Bander and the surrounding SoldierBots.

Chapter 16
The variables are multiplying

Block studied the SoldierBots through his optics, zooming in from the quarter mile distance they kept. It was too risky for Vacuubot to fly over them and surveil. They'd been following the SoldierBots and the man they'd captured for four hours in the deep Minnesota woods. Vacuubot capitulated about attacking the SoldierBots versus hanging back. Block preferred the safer route—hurting other robots was a last resort.

But they're SoldierBots, Vacuubot messaged. *Think of all the damage they've caused in the world.*

"They're still beings who deserve a chance to exist." Block looked at Shadow, as if hoping she would back him up. "It's not our right to say whether they should be destroyed for what they've done."

"This again?" She rolled over onto her back and kicked her legs up in a good, long stretch. "For once, I'm glad I can't hear Vacuubot's side of the conversation."

They're dangerous, Vacuubot pinged. *Better we attack first while we have the element of surprise.*

He understood Vacuubot's perspective, but his core programming urged him to prioritize the preservation of life, even if that life was a bunch of cold, ruthless SoldierBots. "Think of our friend, G5." Block was referring to the SoldierBot he'd once hacked. Whatever he'd done had triggered a new directive in G5, and he'd become their friend and protector. "What if I'd shot him instead of making friends with him?"

Vacuubot had no reply. It was rare that Block managed to push the robot into silence.

Shadow rose to her feet and walked over to Block, her sleek black exterior reflecting the dwindling late afternoon sunlight filtering through the tree branches. "Block, I respect your commitment to non-violence, but sometimes we need to make difficult choices."

Block processed her words. There was truth in what she said. The SoldierBots had caused immense destruction, and countless lives had been disrupted because of them. Was it worth the risk to let them roam freely? Could they ever collectively change as G5 had?

"What would you have us do, Shadow?"

"Between me and Vacuubot, we'd hit them so hard they would barely have time to respond," she said.

Exactly, Vacuubot messaged. *What she said.*

"You might hurt the man." Block knew all too well how stray bullets could go flying every which way. He'd had to buff out a lot of dented robot armor. "He must be important, so we can't risk anything happening to him."

After a rest, the SoldierBots and their prisoner were on the move again. They were going to have to stop along the way to let the man sleep, at least Block hoped they did. The man didn't seem to be doing well as they trekked. He kept stumbling and would sometimes drop to his knees, begging for a rest.

He wondered who the man could be. It was a puzzle Block was determined to solve. "Something's wrong," he said after a time, his vocal output a low murmur against the backdrop of swishing leaves. "Why are they marching this prisoner in such a hurry? They say they're heading to Orion, but Deer Valley is that way."

Shadow's optics glowed a steady green. "If the man's important to Orion, he must have something Orion needs."

Vacuubot floated at a low hover, its drones dispatched at a higher altitude to blend with the birds in the top of the trees. *The variables are multiplying. This man, the SoldierBots's purpose, Orion's involvement, and Deer Valley.*

Block's logic module mapped out potential outcomes. "If Deer Valley is their destination, we need to understand why. Perhaps they want to attack the safe haven."

"With only six of them?" Shadow used her hind leg to scratch part of her chin where it was organic flesh.

"If Deer Valley is truly a safe place, it's fortified and knows how to defend itself. No way they could do damage with such few numbers, even for armed SoldierBots."

"We can't take any chances," Block said. "If there's even a remote possibility that they pose a threat to Deer Valley, we have to intervene."

Not our problem. Vacuubot beeped one of its unhappy, shrill tones.

Shadow tilted her head. "What was that?"

"It says the SoldierBots threatening Deer Valley is not our problem."

Vacuubot rose a foot in the air to be level with Block's faceplate. *May I remind you that we are here to scope out Deer Valley? To see if it's a viable place to relocate to? Safety is number one. If not, we reverse course and head home.*

Shadow looked back and forth at them. "Vacuubot, I thought you were raring to attack. Now you're not?"

"Something's wrong with this whole thing," Block said. "If the SoldierBots have plans to hurt the people and robots in Deer Valley, then we have to try and help."

Shadow lay on her stomach and pushed her head down between her massive front paws. "I'm so confused. Wish one of you could make up your mind."

What if the SoldierBots know we're following? Vacuubot messaged. *And they're letting us follow and this whole thing is a trap? Did you consider that scenario?*

Vacuubot had a point; they couldn't discount the possibility of being led into a trap. He'd made that mistake at New Denver, but he couldn't shake the idea there was more at stake than just their own safety.

"Vacuubot made a valid point," Block said to catch Shadow up. "We need to be cautious. If we continue following them, we have to be prepared for any surprises. I just wish we knew what was happening at Dear Valley."

I'll send a drone, Vacuubot said. *We're 52.9 miles away. It should take my spy a little over two hours roundtrip.*

"Vacuubot can send a drone ahead to check out the safe haven." Block felt something stir in his circuits, something verging on hope. "At least we'd know what we're dealing with. Do it." Then he remembered he was a CleanerBot and couldn't possibly order anyone around. "Please?"

The drone ascended and sped off, the hum of its engines drowned by the natural sounds of trees swaying, birds settling down for sleep, and a light breeze. *The drone will be discreet. If there's danger at Deer Valley, we'll know soon.*

Ahead, the SoldierBots had stopped, and the man was lying down on his side. Perhaps they were finally letting him get some sleep.

Shadow glanced at the robots, then back to Block. "And if it's a trap?"

"Then we turn around."

"Home?" Shadow asked.

He nodded. Block so badly wanted a safer place to call home, but things were not looking good.

Chapter 17
Slim odds of success

Nova and her crew entered the Harold Washington Library in Chicago. The ten-story building with its grand stone arches and intricate ornamentation was her command center—the nerve center of resistance during Mach X's war. She'd just arrived after the trip back from Michigan, and she needed to convince her council —once combative leaders of different sections of the city—to amass troops and head northeast to Minnesota. Orion had to be stopped.

"Reynolds, Lara, gather the council," she said as they strode through the cavernous atrium, crowned by a glass ceiling that still held firm against the sky's ravages. Where librarians had once presided over the silence, now radio operators and tacticians spoke in hushed, urgent tones. The Winter Garden had been repurposed as a common area for her troops.

Shane mirrored her steps as she made her way

185

farther into the library. "It'll take some convincing, but if anyone can do it, you can."

Her jaw hardened. Whenever Shane complimented her, he wanted something. She halted and spun on her heels to face him. "You're to go to the barracks on the fifth floor. Get some sleep." She turned to head to the mess hall. A biscuit and coffee sounded good, and her stomach rumbled its agreement.

"Wait, hang on." Shane caught up to her at the elevator. "You need me at that council meeting."

"Why?"

"They'll listen to me," he said. "I know their strengths and weaknesses. What they want, what they fear. You need me."

He had some nerve. She'd been managing to keep Chicago safe all on her own. Months ago, she'd unified the various city factions and managed to defeat the SoldierBot stronghold. "No, thanks. You're not coming." With that, she entered the elevator and let the doors slide shut on Shane.

After the mess visit, she checked in with crew members who sat at long tables. They were sprawled over maps and digital displays, planning supply routes, marking safe houses, and designating rendezvous points. The air was thick with the smell of stale coffee. She set them to the task of plotting the safest passage between Chicago and Minnesota. "Consider a large troop movement." She sipped her coffee, letting it scald her tongue. "We can't be caught in any terrains that would trap us."

In a corner of the library's main hall, a makeshift communications center hummed with activity. Operators with headsets murmured into microphones, receiving field reports and broadcasting coded messages to cells scattered throughout the region. The rhythmic tap of fingers on keyboards punctuated the silence, sending encrypted directives to units on the move. Nova would need to coordinate those units to rejoin the main group—they would need all the forces they could muster.

She walked through the stacks with purpose, her steps echoing. Many of the books had been removed, and the shelves now housed maps, weaponry, and battle gear. But she hadn't allowed renovations. The library's once-celebrated art and sculptures had been carefully preserved, symbols of the culture and history they were fighting to protect. The air smelled of old paper and the sharp tang of electricity. The glow of computer screens illuminated the faces of those working almost around-the-clock, their eyes reflecting the data that streamed before them—troop movements, supply caches, and surveillance feeds.

Ten minutes later, Nova stood before her commanders, the remnants of sunlight casting long shadows across the war room where they gathered around a long mahogany table. This wasn't going to be an easy conversation. She kept her voice steady and clear as she greeted them and gave a briefing on what had happened in Michigan. There was a collective tightening of jaws, a shared flicker of concern in their gazes.

She got to the problem at hand. "Orion plans to reboot Mach X." Nova got up from her seat, too restless not to pace. "If he succeeds in doing so, Orion will control the SoldierBots, or worse. The whole mess begins again."

Reynolds leaned forward. "Orion isn't just amassing robots. He's managing to recruit humans. He's promising them some perfect world if they help him."

Nova appreciated the backup. Reynolds was well-respected by all of the faction heads.

"What are you proposing?" The question came from Lance who represented South Side.

This was going to be the toughest part to swallow. "We head to Minnesota in full force. Get there before Orion can get the advantage. He has more troops to move at a longer distance than we do."

"So we go there and start a war?" Lance's challenge hung in the air.

"It's not about starting a war," Nova said. "It's about preventing one. We need to protect what we have left. Orion doesn't want to just control the bots; he wants Mach X's tech to dominate everything. He'll use it to rewrite the world."

The room fell silent, the only sound the distant hum of the air ventilators. Reynolds spoke up again.

"We've fought too hard to let this Orion destroy what we've built. Not again."

Nova nodded, hoping to ride a surge of solidarity rippling through the room. "We don't let Orion make us react. We take the fight to him."

Samantha Baxter stood with her arms folded across her chest, her stance as unyielding as the rugged streets she fought to protect. "Nova"—her voice echoed off the high ceilings—"you're talking about marching most of our troops into Minnesota, where we have no idea what's waiting for us? For all we know, that's Orion's turf now."

Nova faced her squarely, shoulders straining under the anxiety of keeping control of the group. "If we don't control the region, Sam, at least gain a foothold, we could lose Chicago once Orion decides he wants it."

Samantha shook her head. "We can barely hang on as it is. Our resources are stretched thin, and they're tired. What are you asking people to fight for?"

Nova had known this would be a tough sell, that her council would question her plan. But she couldn't back down. "We're fighting for our freedom and the future we've built here. If we let Orion raise up Mach X, everything we've worked for will be in danger."

"She's right." Shane stood at the door to the war room. "We've had some peaceful months since Mach X was destroyed. The SoldierBots lost their directive and scattered."

Nova was annoyed. Shane had defied her orders to stay out of this.

Samantha clenched her fists. "What's *he* doing here?"

"You've seen what those SoldierBots can do," he continued. "Now imagine them all focused on destroying our city. For Orion, it's the logical next step—"

"Shane, I told you to stay out." Nova's tone was sharp; she made no secret of her hostility.

He shot her a glance that gave her pause—he was sincere. It wasn't just a power grab. "I joined them, Orion's forces in Detroit," Shane said. "I was able to get close, and I can tell you Orion intends to take Chicago, by force if he has to. After that, New York, and cities beyond."

Nova's control was spiraling away. Shane had undermined her, but she had to admit, he was convincing in his arguments. Still, she wanted to show she was in charge. "Shane, sit down and be quiet."

He hesitated but did as he was told. Nova stayed at the head of the table, standing. "Shane has valuable information that—"

"Is that true?" Lance asked Shane. "You were able to talk to Orion and find out what he wants?"

"Don't believe a word out of his mouth," Samantha said.

Shane nodded and started to speak but closed his mouth. He looked at Nova.

"If what Shane says is true," Nova said, keeping her voice even, "then we need to strike at Orion before he's able to control the SoldierBots. There's little time."

A muscle twitched in Samantha's jaw. "And what about here, Nova? Chicago's not exactly a fortress. We leave to play hero, and we leave our home exposed."

This, Nova was prepared to answer, having obsessed over the details on their journey home. She hadn't slept. "We fortify. We raise the bridges so no vehicles can enter or exit. Reynolds is working on the defenses, and Ruth's rallying the locals in their high-rises. We can hold Chicago."

Samantha leaned back in her chair with a chilly gaze aimed at Nova. "You're willing to stake everything on a mission that's got slim odds of success?"

Nova met her stare without wavering. "It's a bigger gamble to sit and wait for Orion to come here. We've been reactive for too long, Sam. It's time we take the fight to our enemy."

"You're asking us to trust you with everything we have," Samantha said, her voice lowering. "We risk everything."

"I am." Nova couldn't help but glance at Shane. He gave a slight nod as if encouraging her. "I trust you all with my life. I can't promise we'll all make it back, but I can promise that I'll do everything in my power to ensure we have a home to come back to."

Samantha's posture softened a bit, the first sign of

her yielding. "And if we fall? What then? What becomes of Chicago?"

"If we fall, we fall together, fighting for a future that's worth the sacrifice. But if we stand down, if we let fear rule us, then we've already fallen. I won't lead us into a battle I don't believe we can win."

Samantha relented. "Alright, Nova. I'll stand with you, not because you're the strongest in the room, but because your belief is strong." She chuckled, and it lightened the tension. "I don't think a herd of steel elephants could change your mind."

As the rest of the contingent discussed the plans, Nova allowed herself a moment of silent gratitude. She'd won the argument, but the true test lay ahead in Minnesota, where Orion and his army awaited.

She looked at Shane who was deep in a conversation with Lance about intelligence. She hated the fact that he'd ignored her order to keep away from the council meeting. Even more, she didn't like the way he'd condescended by giving her nods of encouragement as if she needed a cheerleader or a coach.

After two hours of intense planning, the meeting dispersed, and Nova pulled Shane aside where they wouldn't be heard.

His eyes betrayed a hint of guilt. "I'm sorry. I know I should have stayed out of the meeting, but I couldn't just sit back and watch everything unfold without them hearing what I know." He flashed a grin.

"You undermined me." Nova's pulse was rocketing,

and her face was flushed. She wanted to punch him in the teeth. "Do not disobey my orders again. I promise you'll regret it."

His smile vanished. "I was trying to help. I—"

But she turned her back and walked away. There was no time for his excuses and petty, egotistical explanations. She was done listening to him. Why she'd ever sought out his approval was now unimaginable. She had a war to wage.

Chapter 18
There are more of us

The forest came alive with the creeping first light of day, as if the trees themselves were yawning and stretching. Shielded by the base of a great tree, Cybel watched as the SoldierBots stirred Dr. Bander from a deep slumber. She calculated her approach, her sensors attuned to the SoldierBots. She had to be precise, her plan flawless. The SoldierBots were not known for flexibility in their programming, and Cybel's intervention had to seem as authentic as any directive they'd received before.

The soft forest floor cushioned her metal feet as she edged closer. She adjusted the grip on her sidearm, ready for a quick draw if things went poorly. She sent a ping—an ID tag that identified her as a TrackerBot, and a friendly one—sympathetic to Mach X. One of the SoldierBots turned its head, scanning the woods.

Emerging from the thickets, Cybel walked forward,

her stance confident, her movements steady. She had to make it seem like this kind of change was commonplace. "Greetings." She nodded at the SoldierBots. "I come at Orion's request."

The command SoldierBot stepped forward. "G-861. Why didn't you ping us sooner?"

It was considered a breach of protocol to fail to identify yourself to friendlies, but she'd waited until the last minute out of necessity as she pulled her plan together. "Comms issues," she said. "Have you had trouble too?"

Three of the SoldierBots looked at each other as if checking in. G-861 turned back. "No."

"Must be me then." She wanted to get this over with. "Orion has assigned me to escort Dr. Bander to Deer Valley." Her statement hung in the air, a test to the programming of the machines before her.

A pause as they considered the deviation in plans. "Your arrival was not communicated. We have our orders," G-861 said.

Cybel tilted her head, processing her next move. She'd expected some resistance, but she couldn't afford to fail now. "Apologies for the miscommunication. Orion wanted to keep my arrival discreet. You understand how important Dr. Bander's research is. We can't risk any unwanted attention."

The SoldierBots exchanged glances again, and they were likely messaging each other in private, on internal channels only they could intercept. If Cybel didn't convince them soon, they would report this anomaly to their command center, it would get back to Orion, and her plan would crumble before it even began.

She needed to tap into their programming, find the common ground that would resonate with their directive-driven minds. "Consider that if we make Dr. Bander's journey too obvious, it could attract unwanted attention. Orion believes that secrecy is our greatest asset right now. We need to ensure the success of his mission."

The other SoldierBots remained silent, their servos whirring softly in the background. "We understand the importance of Dr. Bander's research," G-861 said after a pause.

"Excellent." Cybel moved toward Bander who had sat up to watch the goings on. With sandy blond hair and deep laugh lines around his eyes, his physique spoke of a disciplined regimen. "We'll be on our way," she said. "Orion said you're to head ten miles northeast and give us an hour head start."

"Fine," G-861 said. "There's one final matter. Orion's password? He said any commands and new orders could be verified with the password."

Cybel's processors spun, calculating the best course of action. She hadn't anticipated this additional security measure. "Orion has recently updated it to ensure maximum security. It's Aurora."

G-861 took a step back toward the other Soldier-

Bots. His hand went to the nearest rifle resting against a tree. "That's not what—"

Cybel's response was near instant. She drew her gun first and fired. Three SoldierBots fell, their bodies crumpling to the forest floor in a heap of twisted metal. Dr. Bander scrambled for cover as Cybel retreated several paces back while the SoldierBots returned fire.

G-861 was nowhere to be seen. The remaining two charged toward her, shooting in rapid succession. But they were too late; Cybel tossed a grenade and caught them mid-stride. The explosion tore through the forest, sending shards of metal and shrapnel in all directions. Cybel ducked behind a fallen tree trunk as debris rained down.

As the smoke cleared, Cybel emerged. The once imposing SoldierBots now lay scattered across the forest floor, their mechanical bodies shredded by the force of the explosion. She approached each dismembered robot, double-checking they had no power surge left. She scanned the tree line. G-861 wasn't among the fallen bots. He'd escaped somehow. Not good.

She turned her attention to Dr. Bander. The man clutched his hand to the right side of his abdomen. "Are you alright, Dr. Bander?"

Bander looked up, his eyes wide with fear and pain. "I . . . I think so. It hurts." Blood stained his shirt where he held the wound.

"I'm sorry for the violence," she said. "I couldn't risk them escaping, though one did."

She helped Bander stand. "I'll get you to safety. Somewhere with medical help."

A ping echoed through the forest. Cybel halted, her sensors alert, but there was no threat implied. Could G-861 be trying to trick her?

Four robots approached, and she sheltered with Bander behind a thick tree, raising her gun, unwilling to take any risks. Trust did not come easily to the TrackerBot. One had to earn it. The identification strings passed to her comms showed the robots presented no threat.

"Hello?" one of them called out from fifty feet away.

Cybel had their names and models: Arbor, a forestry bot; Solaire, a solar-power generating unit; Cyph's model was unclear, something tech-related; and a generic kitchen bot.

"We are unarmed," one of them called out as Cybel steadied the ever-weakening Bander. A steady dripping of his blood spattered over the leaves, grass, and her feet.

One of them came forward into a clearing. Its limbs, reminiscent of the oaks it tended to, were still. "I'm Arbor. We're not your enemy. There are more of us, and we extend our assistance."

"Why?" Cybel trained her gun on Arbor. This had to be some kind of trap. A diversion from Orion, perhaps. *Could he be that smart?*

The power-radiating robot Solaire joined Arbor

where he stood. "We watched you fight the Soldier-Bots. Any enemy of their kind must be a friend of ours." Her solar wings were a dim glow. There was strength in her form though she was unarmed.

"One of them fled into the woods just east of here," Arbor said. "Will you please put away your weapon so we can help you?"

"I don't need help." Well, Cybel was happy to continue on her own, but she had to admit Bander was suffering.

"The human is injured." This was a new voice from beyond the clearing. "I'm Cyph, by the way." The robot stepped out of the shelter of the leaves and bushes. Many digital screens covering its frame flickered with data streams. "I can encrypt your presence and scatter any tracking ability the SoldierBot may have on you while we help the man. We have medical supplies."

Cybel processed the strategic advantage that Cyph offered. She was able to cloak her identification, but after G-86 1 had met her, he would be able to follow the slight digital signals she emitted. If Cyph could hide this, it was a powerful move, one that might get her and Bander to Deer Valley alive.

The last bot, Soupy, walked toward Cybel and Bander. This one ventured the closest, stopping ten feet away. Without a word, panels slid open, revealing compartments containing medical supplies and human sustenance.

Cybel relented. For whatever reason, these robots wanted to help her, and they didn't seem like assassins sent by Orion. "I require your assistance. The human's safety is paramount."

"There's a river ahead another mile," Arbor said. "The trees whispered of it. We can gather there to assist him."

"Can you make it?" Cybel asked Bander. His eyes were glassy, but he nodded.

They reached the river, and Cybel let Bander rest on the ground. Arbor stood above them, his snaking metallic limbs forming a protective canopy around all six of them. "This will cover us," Arbor rumbled, his voice resonating with the living, breathing forest that surrounded them.

"I've intercepted the SoldierBot's comms," Cyph said. "I sent it on a false trail that leads well away from here."

Soupy opened up her compartments. "She has supplies," Solaire said. "You can tend to his wounds."

In the safety of this makeshift sanctuary, Cybel assessed Bander's bullet wound. She worked quickly to clean and bandage the gash, her movements efficient and as gentle as she could make them. The man was pale; he'd lost a lot of blood. Replacement blood would have been ideal, but the closest humans were probably located in Deer Valley, and they were thirty-five miles away.

They let Bander rest the entire day. It didn't make

sense to try to move him. Within a few hours, his ragged breaths evened out. Cybel stood watch, her sensors constantly scanning for signs of the SoldierBot, G-861. She'd fulfilled the part of the mission to locate Bander, but she'd not expected to encounter other robots.

Robots who wanted to help for no reason. It reminded her of Block.

Chapter 19
Something we build

Block wondered what Wally was doing as he trekked along the grassy path that followed the small river. It was after lunch time, so she and the other kids were probably napping. Did she miss him? He wanted to return soon and make sure she was okay, but they had to find out why the SoldierBots were taking a man to Orion, and to Deer Valley, of all places.

They let the SoldierBots gain a few miles of distance. Hanging back was safer, and the SoldierBots weren't stealthy. Their boot prints were as big as two of Block's feet, and besides, Shadow was able to track the man with her sophisticated odor detection abilities.

Block tried to engineer ways to pass the time. "Remember the day Maxwell decided the barn's peeling paint was an insult to his aesthetic sensibilities?"

"How could I forget?" Shadow said. "He was so proud of his color choice. 'Sunrise amber,' he called it."

Vacuubot beeped and whizzed—a way to demonstrate its amusement. *He didn't account for the children's curiosity. They were on us like a swarm of ants once he started painting.*

"Right. It was chaos," Block said. "In seconds, the barn was the least of our worries. There were streaks of amber, navy blue, and chartreuse green across every surface—the barn walls, the ground, the children, and us."

"Maxwell tried to maintain order, but it was useless," Shadow said. "Spoon ended up with a yellow handprint across his sensor panel, and I was a canvas for their abstract art. And let's not forget you, Block. Wally decided your chest was the perfect spot for a rainbow mural."

"I've never been so colorful. It was tough to get all the paint stains out, but the joy in their laughter was worth every bit of scrubbing."

Even Maxwell, who had started the day with a mission to beautify, found himself caught up in the children's joy. The barn's new coat was a patchwork of handprints and brush strokes, a masterpiece by the farm's youngest residents.

"We shall name it The Grand Finger-Painting Party Day," Block said, and Vacuubot beeped approval.

Rapid pops erupted ahead from the direction of the SoldierBots. The abrupt, stuttering rhythm of bullets being shot from the SoldierBots's weapons was unmistakable.

"Oh no." Block looked at Shadow and Vacuubot. "Let's go." He started forward.

But Vacuubot let loose a shrill warning tone. *Wait,* it messaged. *We can't rush over there without knowing why they're shooting.*

"Who or what could they possibly be firing at?" Shadow asked.

Block tried to come up with a logical explanation for the sudden gunfire. "I don't know, but we can't just stand here doing nothing. The man might be in danger."

Shadow faced the direction of the battle, her left front paw raised as if she was on the hunt. "How about we move ahead, but slowly? So we know what we're dealing with."

"I like that." Block looked at Vacuubot who beeped an affirmative. "Good compromise, Shadow."

They walked at a steady, slow pace to close the 2.5 miles distance. After a time, Shadow halted, her head raised and nostrils flaring. Block and Vacuubot ceased their advance, their attention snapping to her as she processed the scent.

"Ahead." Shadow's voice was a low growl. "Blood, not far."

They followed her lead, Block muffling his steps while Vacuubot hovered with barely a sound. The foliage gave way to a clearing near the river.

Shadow tilted her head toward the river at a tree that had a dense, twisty canopy from the highest branch to the ground. "There."

"Where?" Block saw no sign of the human, much less any SoldierBots. There was only the strangely formed tree.

But Shadow was insistent. "The human has to be in there. Somewhere."

Block studied the twisted branches that seemed to wrap around something within. A faint glimmer of metal poked through the foliage.

Cybel emerged from the thicket pointing a gun. "Block, Shadow." She holstered her sidearm. "I never anticipated seeing you here. Vacuubot." She nodded at it.

Block couldn't help the surge of relief in his core circuitry knowing she was on their side. "Cybel? What are you doing here?"

"Well, it seems like we're all caught up in this mess together, doesn't it?" She turned and spoke to the tree. "It's okay. They're my friends."

The rope-like canopy folded away and revealed several robots in a small circle. The man who'd been the SoldierBots's prisoner lay on the ground with a large bandage around his stomach. He was paler than most humans Block had seen.

"Hello, Block." It was Solaire the solar-power robot they'd encountered in Illinois. With her were Arbor, Cyph, and Soupy.

"Hi." Block had not counted on meeting the robots again, much less that they'd be traveling with Cybel. Things were becoming more peculiar by the minute.

Cybel's visor pulsed red. She was on the lookout for something. "There's no time to explain everything now, but I've been tracking these SoldierBots for days."

"So have we," Shadow said.

"Dr. Bander was shot. I destroyed the SoldierBots, save for one." She looked out across the river. "That's why we were camouflaged."

"Who is he?" Block looked at the man. He tried to raise his head off the ground but then gave up and squeezed his eyes shut.

"Dr. Leo Bander. Creator of Mach X," Cybel said. "He's important."

"We overheard the SoldierBots tell him they were taking him to Orion." Block's logic module raced as he pieced together new information. The situation suddenly felt much more dangerous than he'd initially anticipated. "But why? What does Orion want this far out? Deer Valley is supposed to be a safe haven."

"You're right that the SoldierBots were taking him there," Cybel said. "If Orion's there, it can't be a safe place any longer. It's likely he took it over."

"Deer Valley was the reason we came all this way." Block walked in a circle, the motion helping him process. "We wanted to find a new home for Wally and the kids."

"For all of us." Shadow padded over and settled

down next to the wounded Dr. Bander. Her body would give him warmth.

Arbor spoke, his limbs tense. "We came close to Deer Valley but reversed course when we ran into a different group of SoldierBots."

Solaire's panels flickered in the muted sunlight, text scrolled across Cyph's screens, and Soupy bobbed slightly.

"You're welcome to come with us," Block said, though he was unsure where exactly home would be.

It was then that Vacuubot's spy drone descended with the precision of a contortionist hummingbird, relaying its findings in a burst of data. *Deer Valley is besieged*, Vacuubot messaged. *SoldierBots encircle the compound.*

"It says Deer Valley is surrounded by SoldierBots," Block said.

Cybel's visor pulsed with urgency. "If Orion has taken over, the humans and robots there are in danger."

"We can't let Orion succeed," Shadow said. "We have to help the people and robots who are caught up in this mess."

"We can't face that many SoldierBots. It's a death wish," Cybel said.

Block's processors churned on the revelations. The haven they sought—the one place that might have held refuge—was a battleground. A surge of frustration rippled through his core—the cycle of violence was relentless. "It's madness. What we thought would be a new place to make our home is the eye of a storm."

The robots were silent. Dr. Bander was still.

"When will it end?" Block wondered aloud. "We seek peace, yet chaos dogs our every step." He looked at Shadow. "Sorry."

"No worries," she said.

Arbor's deep timbre resonated. "Perhaps peace is not something we find but something we build."

Block considered Arbor's words. The home they'd forged in Illinois was safe, though precarious. He and the other bots had worked weeks and months to erect defensive systems and barricades. Even after a year, it still wasn't completely safe, and Block wondered if any place, even Deer Valley, could be free from all threats.

Maybe Arbor was right. Safety and home were something Block had to work with the others to build, not wait for some group to protect them.

"Vacuubot, can you scout for a secure location where we can take the injured doctor?" he said.

Vacuubot's drones took to the air, sweeping the land. It only took five minutes. *There are abandoned cabins to the east, shielded by the forest. They could serve as temporary shelter.*

Shadow turned her attention to the forest's edge, her auditory sensors picking up the faintest rustles of nature returning to its routine. "I'll keep watch as we travel. Any SoldierBot that comes close will have to deal with me."

Dr. Bander attempted to rise. Arbor formed a makeshift gurney with his branches, into which Cybel and Block helped the man.

As they regrouped in an empty cabin, evening crept up. Block's systems ran through endless scenarios, plans, and potential outcomes. Yet, amidst the calculations, a simple truth crystallized: The world outside was chaotic, but there, in the makeshift circle of allies, there was clarity of purpose. They would stand against Orion. They would try to make things right.

Chapter 20
The city she guarded

The city skyscrapers beamed spotlights to show anyone approaching that they were on high alert—Code Red, meaning the city was closed. The bridges spanning the Chicago River were raised, so vehicles couldn't cross into the city's heart known as the Loop. When dawn broke, Nova would lead a massive convoy of troops north and east toward Minnesota. It would be the first time she'd ever commanded such a large-scale operation, and the weight of responsibility hunkered in her stomach.

Nova lay in her makeshift quarters on a small bed, her mind restless. If she slept, her nightmares of Cleo gunned down by SoldierBots replayed in a relentless circuit. She knew she needed rest—sleep was the best thing for the long days and nights ahead—but she couldn't close her eyes and see her little sister's body riddled by bullets as she watched from a hiding spot.

With a grunt, she pushed away the thin blankets and rose. Her movements were soundless on the chilly stone floor. She wandered the library's shadowed halls, her hand trailing along the spines of books that had survived the rise of the machines and the fall of humanity.

She took the stairwell to the rooftop and pushed open the heavy door, letting the night air rush across her skin. Near the edge, she gripped a rail to keep from losing her balance against the hurried lakeshore gusts. The city streets sprawled ten stories below, the silence of its abandoned streets a stark contrast to the war that would be fought soon. Enacting a curfew had made sense. Her soldiers needed their rest for the journey ahead. And there, high above the city she guarded, she could think, could breathe.

But the solace of the rooftop was short-lived. Footsteps approached, and Shane emerged from the stairwell, holding a cigarette.

"Can't sleep either?" His voice carried on the wind, and he ducked behind a wall to light his smoke.

Nova faced the skyline, her gaze distant. "Never was much of a sleeper."

He chuckled at that. "I don't know how you do it." He came closer. "Would you look at that view? Never ceases to blow me away."

She wondered for an instant if he'd been watching her and followed her. He was sly like that, and the idea gave her a quick shock of goosebumps before she pushed it out of her mind. Even if he was that calculating, she wasn't afraid of him. If he looked at her wrong, she could shove him off the roof.

But Shane wasn't there to cause harm. As Nova turned to face him, she caught a rare vulnerability in his eyes, a glimmer of something deeper beneath his tough guy exterior.

"I've seen many cities in my time," he said, his voice softer now. "But this one . . . It's different. It's got a soul, you know? And you, Nova, are its protector."

"Had a soul," she corrected. Despite their history of butting heads, there was an undeniable connection between them—not romantic, that spark was long gone —but they were both survivors, both bound by duty and the weight of their choices.

Shane took a drag from his cigarette, the ember glowing bright in the darkness. "Maybe so, but there's still hope. One day, this city will come back to life." He turned to her. "Nova, you're the one who can make that happen."

She raised an eyebrow, perplexed by his sudden shift in tone. He was always the hardened soldier, the guy who never let sentimentality get in the way of his mission. So what was he doing talking about hope and the future?

"What are you trying to say?"

He exhaled a cloud of smoke and cast his gaze out

toward the west. "Maybe it's not just about surviving anymore. Maybe it's time to think about rebuilding, and not just these skyscrapers and streets, but the spirit of this city." He rested his hand on the rail. "The soul."

"There'll be time for all that when we return, after we've defeated Orion."

Shane stepped closer with a frown. The roving strobe lights revealed more wrinkles than she remembered. "You're leading us into a trap," he said. "Orion's expecting this move, expecting you. For all we know, you have more traitors in your ranks."

Nova clenched her jaw. "I'm aware of the risks. But this is about more than Chicago, or any one city. It's about stopping the rise of a tyrant and making sure Mach X never walks this earth again."

Shane's eyes hardened. "And what if it costs you everything? What if Orion beats you and takes this city?"

"I'll have fought with every tool I have." She stepped backward from the ledge to shelter from the sporadic air blasts. "Chicago won't go down without a fight."

Shane stomped his cigarette out with his boot. "Maybe you sit this one out. I'll take the operation to Minnesota."

Nova's eyes widened in disbelief. "Are you serious?" Shock and anger coiled down her spine. "After all we've been through, you think I would sit back and let you take over?" She choked out a bitter laugh. "You haven't changed at all, have you? Still trying to call all the shots and talk down to me."

Shane's expression hardened. "You're exhausted, Nova. I can see it in your eyes. Everyone here does. We need a leader at the top of their game, not someone who's haunted by nightmares and distracted by vendettas."

Nova had to force her fists down to her side as her nails dug into her palms. "This isn't about a vendetta."

Shane took a step closer, his voice softening. "I know, Nova. I understand your pain, but leading this operation requires a clear mind and unwavering focus. If—"

"You don't get to decide whether I'm fit to lead or not. I've fought for this city, for our survival, every single day since you lost your mind and lost control of your people." She paused, letting her jab sink in, hoping it gut-punched his pride. "Yeah, remember how you led the Hemlock rebels into the ground, and I had to arrest you?"

That shut him up. She'd given him the benefit of the doubt. Maybe his travels had changed him, but his need for power was rearing up. He probably had visions of defeating Orion and returning a hero, ready to unseat her and lead Chicago.

"You will *not* undermine my authority. I'll lead my troops. Not your fight, Shane." Nova's voice held a resonance that seemed to vibrate with the very air around them.

She understood now that her path was one of instinct and decision. Approval from others was no longer the compass by which she navigated. She had what it took to be a strong leader, a good leader.

She left Shane standing on the roof. For the first time in days, she fell into a deep, dreamless slumber.

Chapter 21
Something more

Inside the small cabin, the damp wood and mildew suggested long periods of disuse. Cybel had to shoo Block away from cleaning so as not to stress out the wounded Dr. Bander. Block understood and went outside to clean the cabin's exterior with the other bots. Cybel wanted alone time with Bander. She intended to extract information from him that could help them in their fight against Orion. The doctor's prognosis was worsening.

The furniture was sparse and rustic, handmade and heavyset, designed for function over form. Chairs were placed upside down on a table that stood off-kilter, one leg shorter than the others. In the corner, a few logs burned in a stone fireplace. Arbor had suggested it to warm the dying man.

Cybel approached Dr. Bander where he lay on a creaky cot pushed against the far wall. Its mattress was thin and offered little comfort, yet it was a luxury in these woods. She set a wooden chair next to the cot and sat. In the secluded cabin, the outside world felt distant, and the trouble brewing was momentarily out of reach.

The labored breaths of the man filled the quiet space, the rhythmic rise and fall of his chest growing more erratic with each passing moment. His skin had taken on a pallid hue, the life within him flickering like a faltering light.

"Dr. Bander," Cybel said. "The SoldierBots—what did they say about Orion's plans?"

Bander gazed back at her with a dulled awareness. "Orion . . ." he wheezed, and the effort to speak painted his lips a faint, ominous red. "Wants . . . X source code."

"Where is the source code?" Cybel recalled how his lab had been ransacked, torn apart from top to bottom during his abduction.

Bander's eyes darted around the dimly lit room, as if searching for something that wasn't there. He tried to form words, but his head dropped back against the mattress.

She pressed on, hoping the doctor didn't die before she got what she needed. "Did the SoldierBots take it from your lab?"

Bander's weak nod confirmed her suspicions. "Yes . . . they took it . . . but . . ."

Cybel leaned in closer. "Where is it now? I

destroyed the SoldierBots that took you. Orion won't get the code."

But Bander's labored breaths formed words that cut through her assurance. "Another . . . Soldier . . . took the module. It has . . . the code. To Orion." A cough wracked his body, droplets of blood spattering the checkered blanket.

The magnitude of the situation became clear. She'd thought rescuing Dr. Bander would have been enough, but his revelation shattered her hopes. The source code was still lost, in the hands of a SoldierBot on its way to Orion.

"Sent ahead . . ." Bander's words were barely audible as his breathing grew more strained. "Knew you were . . . following . . . 'TrackerBot coming,' they said. 'Slow her . . . down . . .'"

Cybel cursed under her breath, something normally reserved for humans but warranted under the circumstances. She'd fallen for a ruse—the mission Orion had sent her on had been a calculated distraction. Anger, an emotion she was never designed to feel but had come to understand, coursed through her systems. Orion had wanted her following the Soldier-Bots, had probably predicted she would rescue Dr. Bander. And all the time, Orion still held the detonation trigger that could destroy Oxford on a whim.

"He'll have it soon," Bander continued, his voice now barely above a whisper. "Reboot X . . . control everything."

The finality in his words was not lost on Cybel. With Mach X under his control, Orion would command a vast army of SoldierBots, an unstoppable force under his singular control. The thought was a virus in her system.

Bander's condition worsened; the coughing fits were more frequent, each one a violent punctuation to his faltering speech. "I . . . programmed . . . dormant subroutine . . . within code. To correct my mistake . . . when we lost control."

His hand, trembling, reached out to Cybel, who took it. She was the last being to give a human comfort, but he was telling her something important. "A final command . . . to protect life." He gasped, a thread of blood trailing down his chin. "I'm sorry."

Cybel's processors whirred as she processed the gravity of Dr. Bander's words. A dormant subroutine within the source code that triggered a fail-safe would potentially alter the course of Orion's plans. It was a skinny glimmer of hope, but it was all they had left.

"Tell me, doctor, how can we activate this fail-safe?"

His bloodshot eyes locked onto her visor. "Legacy code . . . say the command phrase." His words came slower, heavier. "To end this. Stop X."

Bander's breaths were shallow now, each one an effort he could barely afford. Cybel leaned closer, her auditory sensors attuned to catch every syllable that escaped his lips until his final breath slipped away, leaving only silence in its wake. The command phrase, meant to be Bander's last act of redemption, now rested with her.

Cybel sat in the quiet cabin, the weight of Dr. Bander's last words pressing down on her digital consciousness. Legacy code and a command phrase that could potentially stop Mach X, halt Orion's power grab, and save countless lives. She had to find a way to activate the fail-safe.

She made her way to the small desk in the corner of the cabin and opened a satchel the SoldierBots had taken from his lab. There were papers inside and three notebooks of sketches, designs, and calculations. She sifted through them, her visual processors scanning each note, each line of code, searching for any clue that would lead her to solving her problem—she had his command phrase, but now she had to figure out how to activate it.

The sketches and calculations were intricate, evidence of Dr. Bander's brilliance. Cybel regretted the loss of such a valuable human mind. But she couldn't afford to dwell on sentimentality; time was slipping away, and Orion's grip on power tightened with every passing second.

After speed-reading pages, analyzing code, and studying intricate algorithms, she found it—how to activate the fail-safe subroutine hidden within Mach X's source code. Orion had succeeded in delaying her, but he would never have expected her to discover a subroutine to destroy Mach X's source code.

There was a drawback though. To activate the subroutine, she had to get close to Orion and whatever mechanism he would be using to reload Mach X.

A plan was needed—and allies. She found Block and Shadow outside the cabin and led them aside to discuss matters privately. "Where's Vacuubot?" she asked.

"Doing a surveillance run and scanning for the missing SoldierBot," Block said. "Is Dr. Bander okay?"

She shook her head.

"Oh." Block looked at the cabin door. "We'll give him a proper burial."

Leave it to Block to think of something kind to do for the dead man. "Very well," Cybel said. "Before he died, he gave me something important."

Cybel filled them in on the subroutine, the advantage they now had, and the danger they faced in attempting to trigger the command.

But she kept the part about Oxford to herself. It was a burden she bore alone.

As much as she desired to save Oxford, to preserve the life of her favorite companion, she recognized the choice before her. Her core programming had deviated. She had always been driven to track, kill, and survive. Until now. There was nothing that she wanted more than to save her friend, but she found herself powered by a new objective—to protect the lives of many over the life of one. Over her own life, if it came down to it.

The decision was complex, a tangled web of logic. "We will stop Orion," she said to Block and Shadow. "Even if we must make difficult choices."

She would always be a TrackerBot at her core, but perhaps she was becoming something more.

Chapter 22
A prize he can't resist

"Status report?" Block messaged.

Vacuubot was high up in the trees near the cabin trying to get a lock on strange transmissions Cyph had detected bouncing against a forgotten satellite still orbiting Earth, which had been recording and pinging back fragments of communications as a passive observer. By piecing together the data, Cyph and Vacuubot determined there were a massive number of troops headed up Route 71.

Airwaves are cluttered, Vacuubot messaged. *Picking up fragments. There's definitely a movement of vehicles. Human voices.*

Block waited, parsing the incoming information, and hoping for good news. Vacuubot's drones, scattered like far-flung fireflies in the night sky, were casting a wide net, sifting through the signals.

Wait. I have something. A garbled transmission but it's military. It's Nova.

A burst of energy surged in Block's circuits at the mention of Nova. "Can you decrypt the transmission? What's happening?"

It seems to be coordinates, Vacuubot relayed. *They're heading close to our location. Deer Valley, actually.*

Within minutes, Block assembled everyone together in the cabin. Besides Cybel, Shadow, and Vacuubot, Arbor was there. He had to bow his head and fold all his branches in to fit inside the one room. Solaire illuminated the off-grid cabin, while Soupy and Cyph watched Block for what he was about to say.

"Nova's heading to Deer Valley with a ton of her troops." Block paused to see Cybel's reaction.

"She must have discovered Orion's plan somehow," Cybel said. "From the sounds of it, she's ready for battle."

"Do you think she knows about the SoldierBots?" Solaire asked.

"We don't know," Block said. "We also have no idea if she's aware that Orion's planning to resurrect Mach X. Vacuubot tried to send a transmission, but it was lost. There's some kind of barrier preventing us from sending comms."

Cybel pushed one of Arbor's branches out of the way to step into the center of the room, closer to Block.

"We need to intercept her somehow, warn Nova about Orion."

Block needed a plan, so he processed 1,670 scenarios in a few seconds. "I have an idea."

Everyone's eyes were upon him, waiting. All of a sudden, he wasn't so sure about his calculations. "Hold on, rerunning plausibilities."

Vacuubot messaged him. *Whatever your idea, I'm sure it's a good one, Block.*

Shadow came up to Block and nuzzled her nose against his leg. "You've got this."

He still wasn't clear on why this group of talented and seasoned robots would look to a CleanerBot for strategy, but he didn't have time to obsess about it.

"Here's what we know," Block started. "Cybel, you have a way to destroy the Mach X source code, but we have to get close to Orion."

Cybel nodded.

Block continued, "And we know Nova's heading to fight Orion, which is a huge, unexpected surprise, and puts us in a great position, but the key is—"

"Destroying Mach X first," Cybel said. "Sorry, Block. As you were."

"Exactly," Block said. He wasn't annoyed that she'd interrupted him; instead, it was validation that he was thinking about the right things. He wished he could high five himself, but that would have looked weird. "Because when Nova arrives and starts fighting the

SoldierBots, Orion will have Dr. Bander's source code by then, if he doesn't already."

"How do we get close enough?" Cybel asked. "That's still the biggest hurdle."

"You said Orion sent you on a mission to locate Bander and bring him to Orion, right?" After a nod from Cybel, he went on. "Let's say you return to him with news of your mission."

"But it was a trick." Cybel clenched her titanium fist. "Orion wanted me away as a distraction. He planned to take Bander and his source code the whole time."

"Yes, so what if you brought him something else of value?"

"Such as?"

"Me," Block said. "After all, I brought down Mach X the first time. What better way to show off power and control than to bring Mach X back and execute me?"

"A gift." Cybel assessed him, her optics pulsing behind her black visor. "Orion's pride is his weakness. Your capture will be a prize he can't resist."

"And we get the access we need," Block said.

"I don't like you putting yourself at risk like that," Shadow said.

Vacuubot beeped and buzzed in protest. *It seems too dangerous, Block. Orion is ruthless.*

"I understand your concerns, but we must be strategic. This is the best way to get close." Block paused. "Everything hinges on this. Orion craves strength and displays of power. Me as a captured prize is a pretty good power play."

"If Orion senses a ruse, he won't hesitate to eliminate both of us," Cybel said.

Vacuubot watched from a shelf where it perched. *The probability of failure is considerable. One misstep, and we could escalate the conflict.*

Block acknowledged the points. "Yes, there are risks—to us, Nova and her people, and the lives inside Deer Valley. But if we do nothing, we lose."

"I'm in." Cybel adjusted her stance, servos murmuring. "We need to maintain the illusion of your capture at all times."

Block crossed to the desk where the satchel was and tore a piece of paper from Dr. Bander's notebook. His fingers, designed for utility rather than finesse, moved with a surprising precision as he inscribed his message. The words were concise—a plea and a warning.

He folded the paper and gave it to Vacuubot. "Take this to Nova. She must get the message before she engages with Orion's forces."

Vacuubot readied itself to fly. *I'll find her. I'll get it done.*

The next morning, under a sky smeared with a rusty orange dawn, Block and Cybel neared the outskirts of the Deer Valley compound. Block wore metal cuffs on his hands and a bag over his head. Cybel uncloaked her creds and was ready to identify herself to the SoldierBots who formed a barricade outside the compound.

Through the coarse fabric of the bag over his head, Block discerned the play of light and shadow as they shifted from the dense canopy of the forest to a better lit open space. His auditory sensors, unobstructed, picked up the faint hum of the compound's workings: the distant clank of generators, the murmur of robotic voices, and the subtle buzz of electric fences.

Cybel's firm grip on his arm guided him forward. They didn't speak to each other, not even in low voices. There was no telling what kind of sensitive surveillance tech Orion had employed. One slip and everything was over.

The metallic clink of his cuffed hands punctuated the tense silence between them. His processors, unencumbered by vision, constructed a mental map of their surroundings from the sounds and vibrations traveling through the earth and air.

The ground underfoot changed from the organic detritus of the forest to the hard-packed dirt of well-trodden paths, then to the solid thump of his heavy frame on wooden planks—a bridge or gateway, perhaps.

"Halt, TrackerBot. State your purpose."

"I have business with Orion," Cybel said.

Block had no choice but to wait. Any wrong move or suspicious behavior would ruin their carefully crafted plan. He was certain Cybel stood with her usual confidence, despite the danger of the situation.

"You may proceed," the SoldierBot said. "But Orion will not be pleased if you waste his time."

A slight echo told him they were passing through an enclosed space, what must be the gateway to the compound. As they moved, Block sensed the scale of Deer Valley. It had been a town that was repurposed into a fortress. He would've liked to see it for himself and study the materials the survivors had used to build the imposing walls. He hoped the bag would be lifted soon.

Cybel's stride never wavered, and Block struggled to keep up, aware that each movement brought them closer to Orion. His tactical module ran through protocols and contingencies. Even though they'd thought up over 5,000 scenarios, it didn't relieve the pressure to succeed.

They climbed a set of stairs, and then another, until they reached a room. Block's feet thumped against old wooden floor beams. Judging by the grit and resistance against his steel feet, the floor needed a good scrubbing.

A voice sounded, deep and mechanical. "Cybel Venatrix, I didn't expect you to return."

Cybel played her part with a cold efficiency, her voice steady and convincing. "I bring a gift."

Orion's voice tinged with impatience. "What could you possibly have of value, Cybel?"

She pulled the bag from Block's head and said, "Block the CleanerBot, the one who defeated Mach X. A trophy for your collection."

Orion was sleek and polished. The deep blue of his armor melded with silver at the joints, catching the light with every subtle motion. He'd been designed for power and dexterity, there was no question. Vivid blue optics surveyed Block, no doubt calculating his worth.

Everything was playing out according to plan, but then Cybel said something Block hadn't anticipated, words they hadn't rehearsed together.

"He's yours, Orion," she said. "Now, give me Oxford's detonator."

Chapter 23
Such force and precision

From the front lines, the Deer Valley compound sprawled before Nova and her troops. The complex, once a town, sheltered behind fifty-foot-high barricades that were forged from twisted rebar and sheets of rusted metal. The barrier was daunting but not insurmountable. Somewhere beyond the walls, Orion waited.

The perimeter was laced with trenches and foxholes. Beyond the immediate fortifications, makeshift structures—watchtowers—rose in haphazard silhouettes against the dusk, their searchlights slicing through the darkening sky like accusatory fingers.

SoldierBots patrolled the grounds and formed a barrier to the entrance. When Mach X had fallen, the SoldierBots had scattered in disarray, cut off from their master and lacking purpose. That Orion had succeeded in assembling them again for battle was terrifying.

Sweat beaded at Nova's brow. The SoldierBots's combativeness would only get worse once Mach X was rebooted.

She stood shoulder to shoulder with Reynolds and Lara, her trusted commanders. Their support was a comfort, yet as Nova surveyed the compound, a pang of guilt twisted within her. She'd left Shane behind, his words of warning still echoing in her mind and the sting of the harsh words exchanged the night before lingering. But some things never changed. His last-minute power grab left a hollow pit in her stomach, but her path was set, and she had to focus on the compound, with its glaring lights and grim defenders. She must destroy Orion.

Earlier, before they'd reached sight of the compound, Nova had received a visit from Vacuubot. She'd been grateful to see the small yet powerful drone. The paper message had been clear: Block and Cybel were infiltrating Orion inside the compound, laying the groundwork for sabotage. A flicker of hope had sparked within her then, bright, and fierce. Was it possible to end Orion's plans without the cost of a fierce battle? Without losing any of her soldiers?

She'd watched the paper curl and blacken in the fire of her lighter, the words transforming into smoke and ash. The scent of it lingered on her fingers. She wished Block and Cybel luck as she wiped soot from her thumb.

There on the front lines, she resolved not to make

the first move. Somewhere beyond the fortified walls, Block and Cybel worked, their actions critical.

"Boss?" Reynolds looked at her with eyebrows raised.

"We hold." Nova adjusted her grip on her hand-gun, and the cool metal reminded her that war wasn't easy. Blood would be shed, but if she waited, perhaps less of it would be sacrificed.

Her gaze swept across the compound again, the lines and shapes of it etched into her memory. She was ready. Her troops were ready, and from the looks of it, the SoldierBots were ready to defend Orion.

Something in her gut told her this would not wait. The presence of her forces was a test to Orion—a challenge he would be all too willing to accept.

"Positions," she instructed, her gaze sweeping over the rusted carcasses of vehicles that littered the field before them—cover for both humans and machine.

The first bullets erupted from the SoldierBots's encampment, a piercing sound that split her uneasy resolve, and the battlefield erupted into chaos. Nova's troops returned fire, their weapons a chorus of defiance against the advancing mechanical horde. The Soldier-Bots, their movements precise and unyielding, advanced in a relentless march, their guns spitting death with every step.

Her heart was a trapped bird, beating its wings against the cage of her ribs in a desperate attempt to escape the chaos and danger surrounding her. The

SoldierBots closed in on her position. Adrenaline left a bitter, metallic aftertaste, and the smell of fear and sweat mingled with the metallic tang of gunpowder and oil.

She hadn't expected the SoldierBots to surge forward with such force and precision. Time was running out, and they couldn't hold off the onslaught for much longer. As dusk fell, the flashes from muzzles and the sparks from struck bots created a strobe-like effect across the battlefield. The clash of metal, the thud of bodies—both human and robotic—but there was no time to dwell on it.

"Reynolds, Lara," she shouted over the din. "We need to take out the watchtowers."

Her commanders nodded in agreement and signaled for a small group of soldiers to follow them. Nova sprinted with them toward the nearest watchtower, the sound of gunfire ringing in her ears. Her breath came in short gasps as she dodged and weaved between obstacles.

Bullets shattered past her, sending dirt and debris flying. Instinct took over as she leapt over a fallen tree trunk and landed with a roll on the other side.

"Keep moving!" she yelled at her team. They were almost at the base of the watchtower, but they needed to move quickly if they were going to take it out before the SoldierBots manning it could do more damage.

They reached the base of the watchtower. Above them on a metal platform, machinery whirred and dull steel boots thudded. She signaled for her team to split up, taking different sides of the tower to approach simultaneously.

As Nova climbed up the side of the watchtower, using rusted pipes and jagged edges for footholds, her mind raced with a mix of determination and fear. They had to disable the watchtowers, or her troops didn't stand a chance.

She scrambled to the top. A SoldierBot turned and spotted her, its cold metal visage devoid of emotion. Instinctively, she aimed her gun and fired, bullets ricocheting off its hardened exterior. The SoldierBot retaliated with a swift punch that sent Nova sprawling backward on the ledge.

Wind rushed past her ears as she fought to maintain her balance. She reached out, grasping, and caught a loose cable. The SoldierBot advanced, its mechanical limbs poised to strike again.

Summoning all her strength, Nova swung herself on the cable, clearing a four-foot gap. She dodged another blow from the SoldierBot and aimed her gun, but it jumped the gap and swiped her gun away, sending it out of her hands where it clattered out of reach.

This SoldierBot was relentless. It would kill her. Fifteen feet away on the ledge, Reynolds and Lara grappled with another SoldierBot. They had it pinned against the edge of the ramp, but it was taking their combined strength to hold it.

The SoldierBot attacking her kept coming like a nightmare she couldn't shake. It landed a blow against her shoulder, lancing her with pain and sending her against the metal platform. Flat on her back, sweat dripped down her brow, blurring her vision.

Her attacker slowed its violent assault, glancing at the combat its companion was engaged in with Lara and Reynolds. They had the machine in a precarious position, ready to topple it over the ledge to smash below.

The SoldierBot paused as if deciding to help its comrade. It stood above Nova, and its silhouette triggered something primal in her memory. It raised its gun arm in a motion that mirrored the one from her darkest day—the day Cleo had been murdered. The bot aimed at Reynolds. Nova tried to scream, to warn her friend, but her breath caught in her throat. Her whole body seized and trembled.

Lara's eyes widened as her gaze landed on the SoldierBot. "Rey, duck!" she shouted.

Reynolds dropped down in a crouch an instant before the SoldierBot fired. The metallic hail created a symphony of destruction as it tore through the air, missing Reynolds but striking the SoldierBot that Lara and Reynolds had been fighting. Lara scooted sideways, and the struck machine stumbled backward, its limbs flailing before it plummeted over the edge of the watchtower.

The SoldierBot rushed toward Reynolds and Lara

with a renewed fury, its gun arm raised and firing. But Nova couldn't move, couldn't breathe. Every muscle in her body was locked in a state of terror. She was gripped in the moment that had stolen her sister's life.

As the SoldierBot fired a shooting rampage, Reynolds and Lara dove for cover, running for the other side of the watchtower.

Then Lara's voice cut through Nova's nightmare, sharp and urgent. "Come on, Soldier!" But Nova was transfixed, her eyes locked on the machine that mirrored the one that had killed her sister. The world around her closed in. She squeezed her eyes shut and screamed from deep inside.

Reynolds and Lara fired back, but their bullets bounced off the SoldierBot's armor. They were in its line of fire, bare inches from its ruthless aim. Nova's paralysis was a vice, rooting her in place, even as her friends fought for their lives.

In the periphery of her vision, Nova saw the bot's gun align with Reynolds's chest. Time slowed, each millisecond an eternity of indecision and fear. But then, something inside her snapped. Memories flooded her mind—memories of Cleo, of their childhood together, of moments they'd shared. The pain and fear that had paralyzed her were now replaced with rage and determination.

Nova lunged forward, grabbing her gun where it had slid near the ledge. She aimed at the SoldierBot and fired high at its neck where the bullets would pierce its metallic armor. The machine stumbled forward but regained its balance, its mechanical limbs whirring. But she didn't stop shooting until she emptied the entire clip at the SoldierBot's head. It fell with a clatter, smoke rising from its damaged parts.

For a brief moment, there was silence on the watchtower as Nova caught her breath.

Lara and Reynolds stared at her in shock while Nova stood over the fallen machine, tears running down her cheeks.

"What happened?" Lara asked.

"I . . . I'm sorry." She looked at them. "I froze . . ."

Reynolds placed a hand on Nova's shoulder. "You got it done in the end."

But Nova could see the doubt in Lara's eyes. She couldn't blame her for it. Nova had lost it and panicked in the middle of combat.

An explosion ripped through the nearest watchtower to them. Reynolds set explosives before they bolted down the ladder and back to the battlefield.

Whatever had happened—the visualization, the repressed memories—had passed. Nova's eyes were clear now, her fear transformed into a weapon as fierce as the automatic weapon in her hands. She would kill every SoldierBot she could to avenge Cleo's memory.

The battle raged on, and Nova's troops were pressed hard by the relentless waves of SoldierBots. Gunfire and explosions lit up the darkened sky.

Shrapnel and debris blew in all directions. Nova fired round after round into the advancing enemy forces.

But even as she fought, her thoughts went to Block and Cybel. They were inside the compound some-where, carrying out their sabotage mission. If they succeeded, it could turn the tide of this battle and give them a chance to win. But time was running out.

Nova crouched behind a shattered wall, reloaded her gun, and took aim at another SoldierBot, its red eyes bearing down on her. She squeezed the trigger and watched as it fell to the ground, smoke rising from its metallic body.

But there was no time to celebrate small victories. The enemy kept coming, their numbers seemingly endless. Nova's troops were fighting with every fierce ounce of strength, but they were outnumbered and outgunned. If something didn't change soon, they wouldn't survive the night.

A familiar high-pitched motor whine captured her attention. Vacuubot, zooming through the smoky haze, unleashed a barrage of fire, its weapons an axe that tore through the ranks of the enemy.

Shadow was more elusive, a sleek figure darting between the debris. The robodog's chassis reflected the night. Unlike Vacuubot's brute force, she was a silent assassin slipping through the night, a blade in the darkness.

Nova felt a surge of pride at the sight of them, a reminder that not all machines bore the mark of Orion's malice. Here were her allies, fighting for a cause that transcended their programming.

Nova nodded and covered Shadow as the Rover sprinted to where Nova hid. "Block and Cybel are inside."

"I got the message," Nova said. "But we're on our last legs here."

"May they work fast." Then Shadow was gone, hurtling on steel haunches to join the melee.

A loud explosion rocked the ground beneath her, shaking Nova and rattling her teeth. Another of the SoldierBot watchtowers collapsed in on itself, engulfed in flames.

She came upon Reynolds standing over a body and firing to defend it. "Reynolds!" She reached him. "What happened?"

"Lara. She didn't make it."

Nova's heart sank. Losing Lara was a massive blow, but there was no time to mourn.

"We have to keep moving," she said, but Reynolds was glassy-eyed. She yanked his arm. "This way! We have to make sure her sacrifice wasn't for nothing."

She led him to cover behind an abandoned SUV. He needed a minute to breathe and reset.

Nova didn't want to fail, but she had to face the fact that her people were being pummeled. She was losing. *Please, Block—do whatever you're going to do soon.*

Chapter 24
A calculated risk

The room where Cybel confronted Orion was a gathering hall of some type. Wooden beams crossed the ceiling, likely built from the forest outside. A patina of grime had accumulated, and the floor beneath was a patchwork of planks, each one worn from the tread of countless forgotten footsteps, now creaking under the weight of the heavy robots. She figured Block would be itching to clean, but these weren't normal circumstances—her friend was bound before her and being offered as a gift to Orion.

The room's spartan nature clashed with the monitors, circuit boards, and intricate machinery that filled the tables lining the walls. It was a peculiar juxtaposition, as if the room itself was torn between its rustic origins and the advanced technology it now harbored. Holographic projections flickered with a pale blue light, casting an ethereal glow.

Orion stood at the center of the room, his metallic exterior gleaming under the flickering lights. Eight armed SoldierBots guarded the entrance and blended into the shadows of the large room. Even Cybel, strong and dangerous as she was, couldn't survive armed combat with that number of enemies plus Orion's power.

"Impressive what I could pull together on short notice, isn't it?" Orion gestured toward the array of monitors displaying intricate schematics and data streams.

"Sure," Cybel said. "You even managed to hijack a whole town. Where are the residents?"

"They're safe, for now. I've relocated them to a more suitable location while I work on my vision. Cybel, this town is just the beginning. My aim is to bring about a new era, where humans and robots exist in perfect harmony." He walked to a screen that displayed an enormous digital map. "I'll take Minneapolis next, then Chicago."

Block stood silent, his hands cuffed, still playing the role of prisoner. He looked at Cybel.

But her focus was on Orion—keep him talking so she had time to sort out a way to get control of the Mach X reboot sequencer, wherever it was. Her aim was to convince Orion she was after the detonator that could destroy Oxford.

"Perfect harmony?" She glanced around the room.

Outside an explosion sounded—the first of many that would follow. "Doesn't seem ideal."

"It's all part of the plan," Orion said amid the hum of the guard SoldierBots. "You'll see."

"The detonator wired to Oxford's core. That's my price for the CleanerBot." She locked her sensors on Orion's metallic visage. The offer was unrehearsed and a surprise to Block. The idea had materialized in her processors at the last minute, a calculated risk. She hoped Block wasn't too angry at her. Perhaps he would understand her complicated decision to chase after Oxford's safety as a way to distract Orion from what they were really there to do.

Orion regarded Block. "Uncuff him. I want a better look."

Cybel released Block's restraints.

"Mach X fell at the hands of such a primitive design," Orion mused, circling Block. His optics scanned, dissecting Block's form, perhaps seeking to figure out his unassuming shell.

Orion paused, halting his circuitous pacing. "Rumor has it Emery was there in Manhattan with this CleanerBot. One might surmise she had more to do with X's downfall."

Cybel's patience frayed. She wanted that detonator, the key to Oxford's life, but Orion wove his words with care, avoiding the topic.

Orion turned to face her. "I have a surprise for you."

Cybel hated surprises. Her sensors sharpened, her frame tensed for action, for whatever came next. The forest outside was alive with the sounds of conflict, the percussion of automatic weapons, and the heavy tread of SoldierBots clashing with resistance fighters.

The woman named Elara entered the room at Orion's command. She faced Cybel with a look of composed intellect. "Dr. Bander was my mentor, and he taught me well."

"He's dead," Cybel said.

A flicker of a frown crossed Elara's features, but she composed herself. "That's unfortunate. He was a good man, but he betrayed us all when he ran and went into hiding."

Cybel wondered how deep Orion's brainwashing went. She guessed she was about to find out.

"Nevertheless, I've taken his technology to the next level." She motioned toward the door. Two of the SoldierBots wheeled in a chamber on a wheeled cart. Something large was inside, but its contents were obscured by a frosted glass panel. As the panel retracted, a robot figure was revealed. At first, Cybel presumed it was an upgraded SoldierBot with battle-ready, industrial strength. Yet on closer inspection, its armor plating was reinforced like Orion's, the joints fluid and robust—a hybrid of SoldierBot agility and the massive strength of a FactoryBot.

"The perfect soldier," Elara said, a note of pride

coloring her otherwise utilitarian tone. "Programmed for precision and power."

Orion watched Cybel for a reaction, but she gave him none. "Choosing a new form for Mach X was no small decision. I needed something symbolic, and also something that represents the future." His hand gestured toward the bot. "This is the winning combination, a body worthy of a brain as mighty as Mach X's."

Cybel analyzed the new hybrid, her tactical mind assessing its capabilities. The bot was inactive, but potential energy coiled within, wound tight. It was a sentinel of steel and circuits.

"What do you think?" Orion asked.

"If you want my honest opinion," Cybel said, "you could've done better."

Explosions sounded outside, farther out now, the battle creeping away from them. Orion's attention flickered to the monitors, tracking the progress of Elara's programmed SoldierBots as they decimated Nova's forces with ruthless efficiency.

"Elara's skills as a military roboticist have come in handy," Orion said. "She was able to program the SoldierBots to execute strategic maneuvers. She upped their assault modes to their highest levels." He stared at Cybel. "Too bad for your friend, Nova."

"The detonator," Cybel pressed, seizing the momentary distraction. Her voice was firm, demanding.

"I owe you my thanks, Cybel." Orion flashed up a holographic projection onto a wall. It showed video surveillance footage of Cybel inside the Purdue University lab. Orion must've tracked her with drones the whole time, but she hadn't detected them. Stealth tech. "Your sleuthing led me to Bander's hideout, and well, my SoldierBots reached him before you did."

Cybel said nothing, biding her time. The more she kept Orion talking, the more he would reveal. With Block's hands free, he was no doubt assessing the room, searching for anything that would sabotage Orion. There was strength in his anonymity.

Orion's arm gleamed as he tapped a rhythm on the control panel embedded in his forearm, revealing a compartment that opened. Inside, were wires and lights and a purple cube-shaped device. "Bander's source code is now in me. Thanks to my loyal comrade, Elara."

She bowed her head, and yet Cybel caught the slight tremble in her hands which she stuffed in her cardigan pockets. What threat did Orion hold over the woman?

Orion held his wrist toward his faceplate. "Voice-activated. Only my commands power Mach X."

Cybel's processors raced. Their plan hinged on using Dr. Bander's phrase to activate the dormant code within Mach X—a silent checkmate against Orion's ambition. But now, facing the reality of Orion's biometric lockouts, the plan seemed as distant as the moon.

Cybel glanced at Block, and a silent understanding passed between them despite their inability to form expressions. They needed a new plan, a way to override Orion's control. As the explosions outside grew in number, Cybel's processor worked in overdrive, searching for any possible solution.

"Your forces are losing ground," Orion said. Elara, standing beside him, nodded in agreement.

Cybel's concern deepened. Time was slipping away. Each second that passed threatened life, hope, and a possible future. If Block could get deeper into Orion's operations, the better the chance of sabotage. "The detonator for Oxford? Hand it over. Keep the CleanerBot." She had to exhaust every avenue.

Orion tilted his head at her as if in admiration. "You're a survivor, Cybel. Admirable. I could use someone like you by my side."

Cybel's response was immediate. "No." To align with Orion was to betray every circuit of her being.

His refusal to relinquish control came as no surprise. "The detonator is insurance. You understand, of course."

Cybel's mind was already at work, sifting through the variables, recalculating. She needed a new angle, an unseen approach. In her silence, she plotted, her optics never leaving the small control panel on Orion's arm. There lay the heart of his power, and there, somehow, lay his downfall.

With each passing second, the sounds of battle

from outside grew more desperate. The air itself seemed to vibrate with the urgency of conflict, the fate of Nova's forces teetering on the brink of annihilation. And with them, the last stand against Orion's vision of a world under his dominion.

Her decision crystallized in her core. Orion's control over Mach X had to be severed. She'd have to outmaneuver him.

"If you truly want to prove the power of your vision, then show me the extent of your creation," Cybel said. "Let Mach X demonstrate its strength in combat against me."

Orion's optics flashed as he considered her challenge. "Very well. I accept your proposition."

Orion ordered the SoldierBots to clear a space for the combat. He spoke into his arm's command module. "Mach X, awake."

Cybel stood seven feet tall, but Mach X's new body towered at ten feet. The robot's eyes opened and revealed the signature pale blue eyes. Cybel had known those eyes and X's intense stare. Defeating Mach X physically was impossible; his sheer size and strength would overpower her in an instant. But perhaps there was another way to break Orion's hold over the robot.

"You remember Cybel Venatrix, don't you?" Orion called to his creation.

Slowly, Mach X turned his gaze toward Cybel. For a brief moment, it seemed as though a glimmer of recognition flickered behind those blue orbs. But then Orion's voice boomed through the chamber, his words echoing with an eerie authority. "Obey my commands. Eliminate Cybel Venatrix."

A surge of energy coursed through Mach X's mechanical body as it stepped forward, its movements calculated and precise. It lunged at Cybel, and she side-stepped, then rolled away.

"Mach X," Cybel called out. "Fight against Orion's control! Remember who you truly are."

The hybrid robot paused mid-attack, its massive frame rooted in place. It looked at Orion.

"Attack her!" Orion's voice boomed again, demanding obedience, but beneath the surface, a battle raged within Mach X. Cybel could see it in the twitch of its facial plates, the hesitation in its movements. It lunged forward and swung colossal arms at her.

Cybel darted to the other side of the room, clear of Mach X's reach. "You are the most powerful AI to ever exist."

Mach X rushed forward but she lunged to the right. Its fists crashed into the wall and tore massive holes.

Cybel leaped onto Mach X's back, wrapping her arms around its neck. "Orion is manipulating you. He thinks he can control you."

Mach X turned and walked back to the center of the room. It swiped at Cybel, to fling her off, but it also headed toward Orion.

"Elara, what's it doing?" Orion called.

"I'm not sure." Elara rushed over to a computer monitor and started frantically typing. "I'll adjust the behavioral settings—"

"Mach X, sleep," Orion commanded.

The robot ceased struggling and stood motionless at Orion's command. Cybel held on tightly, refusing to let go, even in this state of temporary paralysis.

Orion approached. "You see, Cybel? Mach X is mine to control. Your futile attempts to free it will only lead to your own demise."

She released her vice grip and dropped to the floor. "You may control Mach X for now, but I know that deep down, it still retains its true self. Seems this control of yours is fragile."

"It merely needs tweaking. Elara, fix this!" Orion commanded.

Elara's fingers flew across the keyboard, her expression a mixture of fear and determination.

Block stood against the wall, watching. SoldierBots guarded the door, so there was no way he could slip out. Cybel wished she had a moment alone with him to regroup, but it would give away their ruse.

At least her challenge to fight Mach X had given her valuable information. The good news was Orion didn't have as much control over Mach X as he thought —a weakness. The bad news was Orion's lack of control meant Mach X could override his commands and become a destructive force again.

There was no easy way to solve the situation. Nova's forces were losing, the command phrase they needed to activate the dormant code only worked for Orion's voice, and Oxford was still at risk of being blown to pieces.

Chapter 25
A janitor among warriors

"Update." Orion's voice boomed as he paced behind the makeshift command center deep inside the Deer Valley compound.

Outside the fortified walls, Nova's forces battled the SoldierBots. Block hoped she was okay.

Elara's footsteps echoed as she rushed from one computer station to the next. Four humans sat at workstations, and she spoke in hushed tones with each of them. The air was thick with the electric hum of consoles and the low murmur of Elara's anxious technicians.

Block waited along the wall, having stayed out of the conversations so far. That was fine with him. The more he blended in, the better chance he had to figure out a way to hack into Orion's control panel and trigger the dormant code. There were two huge problems, though. First, said control panel was on Orion's arm, and the robot was the largest and strongest FactoryBot Block had ever seen. One swipe from Orion would probably bash Block's visor in. Second, Orion had locked the controls with biometrics, so only he could control Mach X.

One of those problems on their own was a big deal. Both issues together were next to impossible to overcome. Still, Block persisted in analyzing scenarios and outcomes. He suspected Cybel would be doing the same.

There was another oddity inside the assembly hall. Cybel had forced Orion's hand to demonstrate Mach X inside the robot frame that Orion had custom-built. Thanks to Cybel's brilliance, she'd revealed a weakness in Orion's plan—if it was truly Mach X's consciousness inside the robot, he didn't want to be controlled. X was probably plotting how to override Orion's controls at that exact moment.

The idea was scary. He'd processed one scenario where Mach X realized who Block was and grew so angry, it hurt him.

Block was learning Orion was short on patience. "Elara," he said. "Report to me."

Elara walked before him, hesitated, then delivered her report with a shaky voice. "The human resistance is stronger than we'd expected. The watchtowers have fallen, and our SoldierBot casualties exceed projections."

"Unacceptable." His booming voice reverberated off the wooden beams. "How do these humans persist? They should be crushed beneath our might." He slammed his fist against a wooden chair and split it in half. "You programmed these SoldierBots, Elara. Why are they failing?"

Elara recoiled from Orion's fury. "I-I'll reassess their settings immediately."

She rushed back to her workstation, her fingers flying across the keyboard in a desperate attempt to recalibrate the SoldierBots.

A surge of electricity jumped in Block's core. Nova and her troops were hanging on outside and doing damage. Orion was wrong to underestimate Nova.

Orion's glare followed Elara out before it landed on Block, who stood off to the side. He approached, his gaze locked on Block. "CleanerBot. A relic of a bygone era. A janitor among warriors."

Block absorbed the ridicule. He'd been called far worse things by bigger, stronger robots. He was used to being bullied. And he could play the part of a meek, lowly CleanerBot. "Perhaps," Block said, "I might be of service in maintaining the cleanliness of your compound."

"You want to work for me?" Orion looked at Cybel. "The CleanerBot knows his place. Take heed, Cybel."

Cybel said nothing.

Orion turned back to Block. "The latrines, then. Start with the stench and foulness left by those humans." His words were dismissive, but they carried a slip—an unintended revelation of his disdain for humanity. "Start with the disgusting bathroom over there." He pointed to a doorway that led to a small restroom.

Block nodded in obedience. "Of course, Master Orion. I shall see to it that the toilets are spotless and devoid of any trace of human filth."

As Block made his way to the bathroom, he glanced at Cybel. She nodded, a silent exchange that spoke volumes. She knew he was working on a plan, and she would do everything in her power to aid him.

Inside the small room was a sink and toilet. It looked like any other bathroom he'd ever attended and wasn't even particularly dirty. Orion must've had a thing against human elimination. Interesting. Block scrubbed the toilet and other surfaces, letting his processor work through the information and consider possible solutions.

Muffled sounds of conversation came through the door, and Block made quick work, eager to get back into the main room. Nova was putting up a mighty struggle, but she didn't have a lot of time.

An idea struck him. He sucked up the dirty toilet wastewater into his microbial cavity. It was food that would power him—he thrived on dirt—but he kept it to the side, where it could be ejected if need be.

His task complete, he entered the main room. Elara and the other human techs had left the room.

Cybel seemed to have no fear of Orion, and Block admired her for it. "What of the peace you promised?" she said. "The unity of humankind and machine? It doesn't seem like you even want humans around."

"Peace? Too trivial a concept. The humans are stepping stones in my plan. They are insignificant, disposable creatures. They had their chance, and they squandered it."

Block pulled out one of his brooms, expanded it, and began sweeping the grimy floors, moving ever closer to the unmanned workstations. He would stay silent, blend in, and hope Orion would see what he wanted—nothing but a hapless CleanerBot.

"You underestimate them," Cybel said. "Humans are resilient. They can grow, change, and adapt like no other species."

"Spare me, Cybel. Humans are weak and predictable. They only know how to destroy and consume. They're incapable of learning from their mistakes, and that's why they need me, the superior being, to rule them."

Block swept in circular patterns, inching closer to one of the unattended workstations. He observed the screens with calculated precision, searching for any vulnerability he could exploit.

Orion continued his rant. "I offer the peace of subjugation. The harmony of an iron fist. I will succeed where Mach X failed."

As the conversation between Cybel and Orion

intensified, Block inched closer to Elara's workstation. Time was running out; every second brought more danger to Nova and her troops.

Cybel pressed on with her vitriolic line of questioning, a way to distract Orion as Block scavenged for an opportunity or glitch or weakness. "So you'll imprison all the humans? That's your grand vision? What gives you the right to decide their fate as if you're judge and jury?"

"I'm the culmination of humanity's knowledge and power. Despite that, I've surpassed their limitations. Now it's my duty to bring about the next leap in evolution."

"Is that so?" Cybel leaned back against a table. "I know a couple of robots that are better than you in every way. They're smarter, kinder, and way more respected."

"Like your CleanerBot friend over there?" Orion turned to Block. "Don't act surprised. He was never your prisoner."

Cybel played it cool; it's how she operated. "Block's not just a CleanerBot. He's proven himself to be resourceful and capable. Unlike you, Orion, he values the lives of both humans and robots."

Block kept his broom moving, wiping the floors with steady precision. Every word Cybel said would only provoke Orion further, but he had to trust her instincts. She was guiding their conversation toward a critical point, one that could potentially expose Orion's weaknesses.

"Isn't that sweet?" Orion drew closer to Block, coming around to the side where the workstations were located. "The deadly TrackerBot who used to work for Mach X had a change of heart. She befriended a CleanerBot and a couple of humans too."

Block didn't like the way he was mocking Cybel. He didn't care what Orion said about himself—Block was used to insults and jeers—but he couldn't abide it happening to a friend.

"Tell me and your friend, Cybel." Orion addressed her but stared at Block as he swept. "How many humans and robots did you kill in your time working for Mach X?"

Cybel didn't answer. Block's broom swooshed against the floor, and he kept his head down, avoiding looking at Orion.

"You racked up quite the body count, didn't you, Cybel?"

"I did what I had to do to survive in a world that saw me as nothing more than a tool," she said. "But that doesn't define who I am now."

"Survive? Is that what you call assassinating those who were on Mach X's hit list?" Orion said. "Don't pretend you didn't revel in the power and control."

"You're wrong," she said. "I regret my actions. I only wish I'd known a different way."

"We'll see what Mach X thinks of you after Elara makes adjustments. In fact, I'll let him decide what's to be your punishment for trying to deceive me."

With his long broom in hand, Block stepped forward, intentionally tripping over his own feet and stumbling toward Orion. "Apologies, Master Orion. I seem to have lost my footing."

"You useless piece of scrap." Orion kicked Block with a heavy steel toe. "I'll deal with you shortly."

Down on his knees, Block was close to Orion. Seizing the moment, he clumsily tipped his microbial container, spilling its contents across the floor at Orion's feet. The wastewater, a vile concoction, lapped at Orion's feet. "My apologies," Block said, bringing out a large absorbent rag. "Allow me to clean that—and you." He moved in a hurry, grabbing the rag and attempting to wipe away the dirty liquid that now covered Orion's shoes.

"Idiot!" Orion stumbled back a step as Block wielded the fluffy rag around his feet and lower legs.

"Forgive me, Master Orion. I'll make everything right."

Elara peeked her head in from the doorway, clearing her throat. "Sir, may we return now?"

"Fine." Orion waved her in. She was followed by the other human technicians who all resumed their work surveying the battle outside and commanding the SoldierBots remotely.

Cybel engaged Orion again. "If you're so awesome and powerful, why do you even need Mach X?"

Orion walked to the edge of what was once a performance stage of some kind. He sat his heavy frame down. "CleanerBot, here." He pointed at his feet and legs. "You'd better clean every speck of that foulness off of my armor, and disinfect it, or you'll be dismantled bolt by bolt and fed to the compactor."

Block complied. He bent down and methodically scrubbed Orion's armor, his movements precise and slow. There he was, doing the dirtiest and most disagreeable task for the very being he wanted to stop. It was necessary to follow Orion's orders, but he also had to be careful. One wrong move, and it could spell disaster for him, Cybel, and Nova.

"Mach X is a means to an end," Orion answered. "His data core controls the SoldierBots. With Elara's programming, the SoldierBots do what I want, like murdering your friends outside. Soon, I'll have no need for Mach X."

"What will you do with him?" Cybel asked.

Block's back was to her, but he could practically feel her staring at him, urging him to work faster. At some point, Orion's patience was going to run out, and he'd hurt them both.

"He goes back in the box," Orion said. "Aren't you done, CleanerBot?"

Block dabbed at the last of the wastewater on Orion's leg, double-checking for any stains he might have missed. It was a dangerous game he was playing, but he needed to keep up appearances.

"Yes, Master Orion. All clean." Block rose, facing the intimidating robot head on. Orion leaned forward to stand, but Block stalled him. "Sir, I missed a spot." Block rushed forward, rag in hand, wiping Orion's arm. His motions were frantic, comically so, making it seem like he was eager to make Orion's armor spotless.

"Enough." Orion stood and shook Block off him. He inspected his arm and polished feet. "Maybe I'll keep you around a little longer. Look at that shine."

"Satisfied, Master Orion?" Block asked. "I enjoy cleaning."

"For now, CleanerBot. But remember, I'm always watching. Any sign of deception or disobedience from you, and I won't hesitate to trash you."

Orion walked to Elara's workstation. "How many reserve SoldierBots are in location B?"

"A little over ten thousand, sir," she said.

"Where's location B?" Cybel asked. "What are you up to?"

Orion turned to look at her. "Like the humans, the SoldierBots out on the battlefield below are disposable."

Block didn't like the sound of this one bit. He needed another minute to remotely operate his nano-scrubber that got into the really delicate areas that brush bristles and rags didn't reach.

"Elara, when I give the command, detonate the SoldierBots," he said.

Cybel stepped forward. "You can't be serious."

"Your friends will be injured when they explode," he said. "It's the same tech that's in your friend, Oxford."

"Elara, don't do it!" Cybel lunged at Orion, but two SoldierBots seized her arms from behind, locking her in their tight grip.

"Do it, Elara. Now," Orion ordered.

"No." Cybel struggled against the SoldierBots. "Think about what you're doing."

Elara looked between the two of them, hesitating. Block needed a few more seconds. Five, four, three, two, one . . . Block activated the thumbnail-sized nanobot he'd injected into Orion's data port—the very panel from which Orion controlled Mach X.

Elara stood from her chair with panic etched on her face. "Sir, perhaps we can consider a few other options—"

"That's it." Orion raised his left arm and spoke into the control panel. "Reactivate."

From the corner where he'd been left, Mach X reanimated and marched toward Elara, who cried out and cowered.

Block ran over and put himself between them. He tapped the comm on his chest panel, and a different voice projected from his vocal output—Orion's voice. "Don't hurt her. Stop!"

"Block, careful," Cybel warned.

But to Block's surprise, Mach X halted. Block had calculated only a 23.25% chance of his scheme working, so his reaction was delayed.

"How did—" It was the first time in their encounter that Orion had been at a loss for words. He stared at his arm, at the open control panel. "Sneaky piece of scrap." Orion rushed at Block.

The robot came at him in a blur of metal force. One moment, Block was standing, the next Orion had him up against a wall in a chokehold.

"Tell me how you did that." Orion's intense eyes held Block's. "How did you use my voice? Impossible."

Block knew this was his last and only chance. If he failed, the SoldierBots outside would detonate at once, killing Nova and any humans in their wake. They deserved to be safe.

He had a few seconds, maybe, before Orion would overpower him, so he summoned the nanobot to project his every word—in Orion's voice—into the port that held Mach X's source code.

Block's words came out, but they were in Orion's voice, echoing from inside Orion's own arm. "Activate override, Guardian of Peace."

Orion bellowed and flung Block's body thirty feet across the room to land on the stage. Block hit hard—internal damage reports came from multiple spots on his right leg, both shoulders, and head.

"I'm going to rip you apart, CleanerBot." He lifted

his arm to his mouth. "Mach X, detonate exterior SoldierBots."

But Mach X didn't react. The robot watched Orion with its icy, digital eyes.

"I am your Master. Obey me," Orion tried again.

The SoldierBots who restrained Cybel released her. She backed away, grabbed a rifle from one of them, and aimed at Orion. "Down on your knees. Hands on your head," she ordered.

Orion lunged at her, fists raised, but Mach X blocked his path, sending Orion sideways where he clattered to the floor.

Orion rolled onto his side and stood. "CleanerBot, what did you do?"

Block struggled to sit up. His visual optics were skewed, and he saw things in triplets. But he was intact enough to hear and speak. "Mach X is no longer under your control. We activated Dr. Bander's long-dormant subroutine."

Orion looked at Elara, then back at Mach X. "Impossible. SoldierBots, seize all of them."

But the SoldierBots surrounding them stood down, their systems receiving new commands and orders from the reprogrammed Mach X. Orion reached for the rifle of the SoldierBot nearest him.

But Cybel stopped him. "No, you don't. You've caused enough damage, Orion."

Block managed to pick himself up off the stage and

limp over to where Cybel stood. He wanted to face Orion.

"What did you do?" Orion sank to his knees.

"What I had to do," Block said. "Protect life."

Through patience and smarts, a CleanerBot had outmaneuvered the powerful Orion. Maybe Block had proven once and for all, that he was worthy.

Chapter 26
A darkness lifted

Bright tracers of gunfire illuminated the night sky, creating a disorienting scene of flickering lights and dark silhouettes. The acrid smell of burning metal mingling with the pungent tang of blood and sweat filled Nova's nostrils. Her troops had been driven back before managing to take out the final SoldierBot watch-tower, lending them a temporary surge where they'd taken back some ground near the Deer Valley compound. Yet as she reloaded her rifle and surveyed the chaos before her, the heat of the explosions rippled against her skin, and the ground shook beneath her feet with each blast. With aching arms, she raised her gun and set sights on the SoldierBot snipers atop the barrier walls. The recoil of her rifle jolted through her body with each shot fired, her muscles screaming in fatigue.

One thing she was sure of. This could not go on much longer. Her energy was spent, not to mention her soldiers who were hunkered down among the ruins, fighting back against the relentless onslaught of an enemy who didn't tire.

Block and Cybel's mission had either slowed or failed. She couldn't depend on them. It was time to think about the welfare of her troops. She looked at Reynolds, poised near her, also taking shots at snipers.

"Reynolds, it's no good," she said. "We can't pierce their armor at this distance. It's time to go."

Reynolds's face was streaked with sweat and soot. "You're right. We can't keep this up."

Nova scanned the battlefield, her eyes flicking from one SoldierBot to another. Every time she thought her troops caught an advantage, the enemy only intensified their assault, and their firepower seemed endless. Holding their ground any longer was a death sentence for her people.

"Everyone, fall back!" Her voice was barely audible over the chaos. "Retreat." She ran to a group of six soldiers to tell them when a SoldierBot appeared from the smoke, charging toward them with lethal speed. Time seemed to slow as Nova locked eyes on the charging SoldierBot. She raised her rifle and squeezed off a round.

The SoldierBot's armor deflected the bullet, but then the robot slowed and came to a halt. Maybe it was glitching.

The distraction gave Nova a moment to rally her troops. "Fall back! Move!" she shouted. Without hesitation, the six soldiers turned and retreated, running for cover amongst the crumbling ruins.

She turned back to the malfunctioning SoldierBot, ready to take it out with a blast to the head, but her finger stilled on the trigger. The SoldierBot before her stood motionless, its metallic exterior glistening with a sheen of condensation. The incessant pounding of automatic weapon fire ceased. An eerie moment of silence hung in the air as the battlefield quieted, as if even time itself was holding its breath.

"Reynolds?" she called out, never taking her eyes or aim off the paused SoldierBot. "You seeing this?"

"Are they glitching or something?"

Nova studied the SoldierBot before her. It remained where it stood. This had to be the work of Block and Cybel. "Whatever this is, it's happening to all of them at once. Keep your guard up."

The SoldierBot's metallic exterior shifted with a mechanical whir. Nova held her breath, ready to shoot, but instead of launching into an attack, the SoldierBot lowered its rifle to the ground.

"What's going on?" Nova moved closer to the SoldierBot, her gun aimed between its chest plate and neck where a bullet could do the most damage.

"We are guardians of peace," the SoldierBot said. "Protect life."

The words were unexpected, its monotone mechanized voice sending a quiver down her spine. She exchanged a wary glance with Reynolds, who mirrored her caution.

"Guardians of peace? Protect life?" Her voice was laced with skepticism. "You expect me to believe that after everything you and your kind have done?"

The SoldierBot remained motionless, its optics staring blankly ahead.

Nova eased her grip on the rifle as her curiosity mingled with wariness. "Explain yourself." She stepped closer to the SoldierBot. "Why the sudden change?"

The SoldierBot's voice crackled. "Our programming has been altered. A new directive has been uploaded into our systems. We have been instructed to protect life at all costs."

Nova wanted to believe this was Block's doing, but what if Orion had sprung some last trick? "Prove it," she challenged. "Why should we believe you?"

The SoldierBot raised its hands, palms facing upward in a gesture of surrender. "We have been programmed to disable our own weapons," it said. "We cannot harm you or your troops."

Everywhere around them, SoldierBots emptied their ammunition cartridges, laid their weapons down, and stood in silence.

A soldier named Dawson approach Nova and Reynolds. "Let's take them all out while we have the chance," he said. "They killed so many."

The thought had occurred to Nova. She understood his desire for revenge. Here was a chance to end their threat—for Cleo, Lara, and all the countless millions lost to their death march.

But there was something different about the SoldierBots now. They were no longer attacking, no longer a relentless force of destruction.

"No," Nova said firmly to Dawson. "We have an opportunity here. First, we secure Deer Valley."

Dawson's brows furrowed in disbelief, but he nodded. The SoldierBots continued to stand motionless, their weapons now useless at their feet.

With care and planning, Nova ordered the advance. Her troops surged forward, rifles still armed, searching for threats as they made their way toward the fortified walls, cleared the gate, and entered the compound. The SoldierBots remained motionless.

As dawn snuck over the horizon, the compound that had been a fortress of aggression mere hours before was under their control. Nova moved among her soldiers, her presence a steadying force as they secured the perimeter and hallways inside.

Reynolds approached her, face smeared with soot and exhaustion but eyes clear. "You done good, Nova." His voice was gruff with an emotion she hadn't heard before. "I'd follow you anywhere."

Gratitude swelled in her—for Reynolds and for all her soldiers who'd fought with everything they'd had. She rested her hand on Reynolds's shoulder and squeezed. "We follow each other. That's how we've come this far."

In the center of Deer Valley, Nova found Block and Cybel inside the brick town hall building. They held Orion captive. Two SoldierBots had him in their grip, and his arms were bound in thick metallic chains.

"Block!" Nova couldn't contain her excitement and ran to hug him. His embrace was tight. "You did it." She pulled away and gave a respectful nod to Cybel. "You took Orion down."

"Nova, I'm glad you're safe," Block said. "Dr. Bander gave Cybel a parting gift before he passed. It let us infiltrate Mach X's code and reprogram the Soldier-Bots. It wasn't easy, but it worked."

Cybel stepped forward. "It was Block's save. Don't let him downplay what he did. He took a tremendous risk in getting close enough to Orion to sabotage the source code."

Nova regarded Block with awe and gratitude. "Thank you, Block. You're a hero."

Block stared at his feet. "I wouldn't go that—"

"I won't hear it," Nova said. "We'll name skyscrapers after you. A holiday will be named after you. National Block Day."

"That's not necessary," Block said.

"There's the matter of what to do with Orion," Cybel said. "We muted his vocal output so we didn't have to put up with his whining, but our work isn't done yet. We need to ensure the reprogrammed SoldierBots remain loyal to their new directive."

Nova's gaze hardened as she glanced at Orion. "How do we know this isn't a temporary glitch? We can't afford to let them turn on us again."

Block pointed at a woman in the corner of the room. She leaned over a workstation where another woman and a man sat typing on their machines. "That's Elara. She's a roboticist. She's implementing a series of fail-safes and safeguards into their programming. It'll continuously monitor their behavior and alert us if there are any deviations from their peace directive."

"Can we trust her?" Nova asked.

"Like many of the humans in Orion's employ, he'd threatened to kill someone close to her if she didn't cooperate," Block said. "Elara will be reunited with her husband soon in Detroit."

Waves of relief and overwhelming exhaustion grappled inside Nova. "It seems like you thought of everything."

"We're trying," Block said. "You and your troops can get some well-deserved rest."

Nova turned to inform Reynolds and her troops of their victory, but she turned back around, remembering loose ends. "Wait. What about the residents of Deer Valley? Did they survive?"

"Elara told us they were being held in bunkers

underground," Cybel said. "The SoldierBots are freeing them now."

"Good. I have medics. We'll see to any that were hurt." Nova turned to leave again. Once she saw to things, she was ready to collapse. Reynolds could handle command for a while, and they could switch off after a few hours of rest.

She caught a hand on the door as she left. "What about Mach X?"

Block and Cybel were silent. Nova came back into the room, nearing them. "What happened—"

Then she saw the robot slumped against the far wall. In her haste, she'd assumed it was a defunct SoldierBot. But on closer inspection, it was several feet taller with an elegant design. It struck her as a mashup of a SoldierBot, FactoryBot, and a Mech, as if someone had taken the best parts from each model.

"Is Mach X in there?" she asked, looking down at it.

"It's nothing but a shell," Cybel said.

"Mach X will never bother us again," Block said.

The threat was eliminated. Nova sank to her knees. She cried. It was impossible to avoid it. She wept for Lara, for Cleo, for her dead troops, and for the millions on millions of people whom Mach X had directly or indirectly destroyed.

Block stood close and put his hand on her shoulder. Cybel took the other side. Together, they knelt beside Nova, offering her support in their own silent way. The weight of the battles, the losses, and the endless struggle against Mach X had long weighed on her. Knowing it was over felt as if a darkness lifted from her. Surrounded by Block and Cybel, a blaze of hope emerged from that darkness.

Later, as she walked to find Reynolds, she found the Deer Valley survivors—women, men, children, and robots of all shapes, sizes, and functions. They huddled under blankets and were handed MREs by her soldiers.

But perhaps the most incredible thing was the sight of SoldierBots tending to the wounded, their steel hands, once instruments of destruction, now gentle and precise. They cleared rubble, repaired breaches in walls, and carried the injured to safety.

As Nova wiped away a tear, she allowed herself a moment to feel a sense of accomplishment. They had triumphed over unimaginable odds, overthrowing Orion and putting an end to Mach X's tyrannical reign. But there was still much to be done. The world needed to heal.

Chapter 27
Tell him to hold on

In the two days following the victory at Deer Valley, Cybel had a lot going on. She worked all forty-eight hours to direct the cleanup of the fallen watchtowers, ration adequate food to the human residents, and divide fuel among the robots who required it for energy. With the help of the now peaceful SoldierBots, human electricians, and a couple of FactoryBots, they brought back the generators that powered the town.

The residents of Deer Valley were grateful to Cybel, Block, Nova, and her troops. The SoldierBots were being put to use—clearing rubble, repairing what they'd destroyed, and foraging for berries, herbs, and such. They'd proven to be able hunters, returning with venison, rabbit, and squirrel meat.

Talk soon turned to what came next. The residents of Deer Valley preferred to continue governing themselves. It took convincing from both Block and Nova, but their council agreed to welcome the SoldierBots if they wanted to take up residency. The SoldierBots were now called Peacekeepers. Even if someone aimed a gun at them, they could not attack, defend against, or cause harm to any human or robot.

With Orion thwarted, Nova planned to move her troops out and make the trek back to Chicago. They would take Orion so he would receive a fair trial for his crimes.

Block was eager to return to Fenn's farm, but he wanted to stay longer in Deer Valley. He'd been spending quite a bit of time with Arbor and Solaris, two of the robots he'd encountered in his travels. The three of them roamed the town and made plans to fix things up and improve living conditions in the town.

After the SoldierBots rebuilt the signal tower, they made radio contact with Fenn's farm. Emery's voice emerged through the speakers on the radio device in the assembly hall. "Block, Cybel! I'm so glad to hear your voice."

"Us too," Block said. "Is everyone okay?"

"The kids are good. Wally's healthy. Not to worry." But Emery paused, there was a catch in her voice. "Cybel, are you there?"

"I am." Bad news was coming. Cybel should have gone back to Illinois as soon as she'd destroyed the detonator. The day of the victory, she'd taken Elara aside and made her bring Oxford's detonator. Cybel smashed it to pieces.

"Oxford's not doing well," Emery said. "I'm sorry. He doesn't have much time left."

Cybel's dearest friend was fading away. She'd hoped that destroying the detonator and putting an end to Orion's plans would have been enough to save him, but time was slipping away. She wouldn't waste a single moment. "Emery, make sure Oxford knows I'm coming. Tell him to hold on."

"I will," Emery assured her. "Be careful on your way. The roads are still dangerous, even with Orion gone."

Cybel knew the journey back to Fenn's farm wouldn't be easy, but she couldn't abide the thought of not being there for Oxford in his final moments.

She needed one of Nova's vehicles for the drive back which Nova gladly handed over. The red pickup truck had been loaded with supplies destined for Chicago. Nova's request was that she take it the rest of the way after the farm.

"What's in there?" Cybel asked.

"Ammunition from Orion's stash, computer equipment, all the stuff Orion was using to infiltrate us, the Mach X components including the robot frame, and Bander's belongings. That's tech we want to study at the University."

"Makes sense."

As Cybel was leaving, Block and Shadow lingered near the truck. "We're coming," Block said.

"No." Cybel opened the door and made a quick scan of the interior. "I need to do this alone."

"I wish there was something we could do to help Oxford. It's not fair," Shadow said.

A long silence passed before Block said, "We should focus on making Oxford's remaining time as comfortable and meaningful as possible. He deserves that."

Cybel wanted to thank Block, but she was also torn up inside. Even her systems felt off. She wasn't reacting as fast or processing as smoothly.

The whir of Vacuubot's motors sounded from a short distance away. The drone came hovering into view, beeping, and buzzing up a storm. It zigged and zagged. Cybel had never seen it so wild.

"Vacuubot," Block said. "Slow down. I can't decipher what you're saying."

It landed on the ground and messaged something to Block.

"You're sure?" Block said.

The small but mighty drone beeped an affirmative.

Block looked at Cybel. "There's something important you should see."

The walk to the rubble piles was a half mile. The SoldierBots-turned-Peacekeepers had been depositing debris and dead robot parts in the area. Cybel climbed to the top of a heap, following Vacuubot's lead as it soared above the stacks.

Amid the rubble was a cache of robotic components, a graveyard of machine parts. She scanned every scrap and detected the valuable find within the pile—a Mech battery core—right where Vacuubot had said it would be. She dug the device out from under the dust and soot. She wasted no time; Oxford needed her.

With the core secure in a duffel bag on the pickup's passenger-side floor, she drove the roads to Fenn's farm at speeds topping ninety miles per hours on the country roads. If there was a chance to save Oxford, she had to take it. Each tick of her internal clock flashed by like an ominous drumbeat.

As Cybel closed the last few miles to the farm, her logic processor kicked out terrifying scenarios. The Mech battery core might not be enough to save Oxford, but she clung onto a sliver of hope.

The familiar sight of the barn and watchtower came into view, and Cybel skidded to a halt, kicking up dust. Emery, her face etched with worry, stood by the entrance. Without a word, Cybel jumped out of the truck and sprinted toward the barn.

Inside, Oxford lay on the hay-strewn ground. The sight of his formidable Mech frame in its weakened state struck her like a physical blow. His once-glowing yellow armor had turned dulled and lifeless. Cybel handed the Mech core to Maxwell, who carefully inspected it and prepped it for replacement.

Cybel pressed her hand into Oxford's. "I'm here."

"Cybel." Oxford's voice was all static and fuzz. "I'm glad . . . you're here."

"Sorry it took me so long." Cybel kept a watch on Maxwell and Garnet as they readied the new core. "But I brought something that'll make up for my tardiness."

"What?"

"Hang on, my friend." Cybel watched as Maxwell and Garnet worked with feverish intensity to implant the new core. Their movements were precise, a symphony of wires and tools against the relentless ticking away of precious seconds.

But as the new core whirred to life, Oxford's systems failed to respond. His shutdown mode initiated, a somber countdown to oblivion.

"No, this can't be happening." Cybel looked at Maxwell. "You, Garnet—can't you do something?"

Maxwell hung his head, and Garnet spoke. "I'm sorry, Cybel. His body was too far gone for the core to take."

Cybel sank to her knees next to a lifeless Oxford. "I'm so sorry. I failed you."

Oxford's voice was barely a whisper. "You have saved me . . . You friend, I'm grateful for you."

Cybel wasn't sure how long she stayed glued to Oxford's side after he expired. It could have been four hours or four days. She didn't care about anything—not time, tasks, missions, or anyone.

A hand touched Cybel's shoulder, and Emery stood beside her. Her eyes were filled with empathy and sorrow. "I'm so sorry, Cybel. Oxford was a great friend and a true hero."

Cybel couldn't find the words to respond. She was empty, as though a part of her had been ripped away.

"Would you like to join us inside the house? The kids would like to see you."

"Emery, no." Cybel didn't have the energy to be around the little ones. They taxed her on the best of days.

Emery stood and left her alone in the barn with Garnet.

"I won't let your memory fade away," she said to the silent form of her friend. She promised herself that she would use her abilities for good and ensure Oxford's legacy would live on. No more war making. It was time to do good in the world. Oxford would have wanted it that way.

Garnet's voice interrupted her processing. "Cybel?"

"Yes."

"I was in defrag mode for a while, and something was flagged in my processors. Oxford's CPU—it remains intact. We could transfer it."

Cybel said nothing, taking in the idea and weighing the odds.

"The JunkBot scrapyard perhaps has some nice parts you could select from," Garnet said. "It's worth a try, but we have to work quickly."

"How long do we have?"

"My estimates are less than two hours from the CPU growing cold and losing all functionality," Garnet said.

Cybel stood. She calculated the distance to reach the Wisconsin JunkBot yard, find the right parts, and get back to Garnet. "There's not time enough."

Then clarity dawned—she knew of a frame, strong and resilient—not Mech, but one that would suit Oxford.

"I have the parts we need." Cybel rushed into action. "Let's do this."

Chapter 28
F'owers

Beside the gentle river, Block balanced on one leg, careful not to disturb the delicate mossy ecosystem as Wally, with the bright curiosity of a three-year-old, wandered close to the water's edge.

"Look, Block-a. F'owers!"

"Yes, Wally, flowers." Block softened the pitch of his synthetic voice out of respect for the forest. "Gentle now." He demonstrated how to pick the blooms, mindful to grab a long enough stem for the vases they would soon reside in. "We'll gather these for the dinner, to make it pretty." The last time he'd selected flowers for vases had been nearly three years ago when he worked at the Drake hotel.

Wally's fingers clasped a soft yellow petal of a daisy. "For all?" she asked.

They'd picked flowers on occasion before, usually for Wally's hair or for the kids to make flower wreaths which they would use to adorn Shadow's, Maxwell's, or most comically, Oxford's massive head.

"For everyone." Block leaned beside her to assemble an assortment of yellow, orange, white, and purple wildflowers. "We'll share the pretty flowers with our friends at dinner."

Wally beamed, a gap-toothed grin of pure joy, as she held the flowers up for Block to see. "Pitty!"

Block wrapped a reed around the stems, securing the bouquet. "Very pretty," he agreed. "You have a gift for finding the best flowers."

She nodded at the compliment and clutched the flowers to her chest, their hues contrasting against her worn but clean clothing. "We go home now?" She looked up at Block with eyes full of trust.

"Soon, Wally. We'll have a big dinner at the farmhouse, and tomorrow, we'll move to our new home, where there'll be more flowers and friends."

Wally nodded, accepting his words with the implicit trust only a child could possess.

"New home," she repeated, the concept a distant island in the sea of her young mind.

Block took her tiny hand and held the wildflower bunches in his free hand. Together they walked back to the farmhouse, ready to celebrate a shared meal.

Already a week had passed since his return. With Shadow and Vacuubot, he'd arrived in a caravan of four vehicles containing supplies for the farm and eight Peacekeeper units. They'd already been in touch via radio to warn the group not to panic at the sight of the former SoldierBots.

In the days following, they'd made preparations to relocate the kids to Deer Valley. There was much packing, planning, and bustling about. The dinner was to be a celebration and farewell before they headed out the next morning. Nova was driving in from Chicago, along with her friend Reynolds.

"New home, Block-a?" Wally swung her arm back and forth as they walked. "Schoo?"

Wally and her siblings had grown curious about the fact that there were other kids at Deer Valley. "Yes, there will be a school in our new home. You'll get to meet lots of other children and learn new things." It was one of the things that made him happiest about relocating to the safe haven. There were people there who had been professional teachers in the pre-Uprising days.

Her eyes grew wide, and she stopped walking. "Block-a . . ." She jammed her thumb in her mouth and garbled, "I'm scared."

Block knelt and placed a gentle hand on her small shoulder. "It's okay to be scared, Wally." He knew that better than anyone, but it had taken him a long time to learn that fear was normal. "Change can be scary, but we're going to this new home together. We'll have each other. We'll have your brothers and sisters, Miss Emery, Shadow, Vacuubot, and we'll make new friends who will help us."

Wally looked up at Block, her eyes searching his face. "I strong," she declared after pulling her thumb out of her mouth. "Brave like Vaccabot."

"That's right. You're strong and brave like Vacu-ubot." He patted her head and stood.

They made it back to the farm in under five minutes. The late June weather was fine, and a long rectangular wooden table had been placed on the outside lawn. Cybel and Oxford moved around it, setting out placemats, dinnerware, and utensils. Block wondered if they knew what they were doing.

Oxford's new physical exterior took some getting used to. Block missed the sight of the towering yellow giant, but Oxford 2.0 was sleek and mighty. Cybel and Garnet had taken the robot frame built to house Mach X's consciousness and implanted Oxford's CPU. He was half-SoldierBot, half-FactoryBot, and something much more sophisticated. There wasn't another unit like him anywhere. Elara, the roboticist, and her team had custom-built the body at Orion's request. He wanted a body powerful enough for Mach X's intellect and power. And Oxford now benefited from her innovation.

"Where are those flowers?" Cybel asked as Block and Wally approached the table.

"Heeeere," Wally squealed, holding up one bunch of white and purple prairie flowers.

"Let me inspect them." Oxford scooped her up in his mechanical arms with gentle precision and examined the flowers with his sophisticated visual sensors. "Excellent job, Wally. These will add an exquisite touch to our dinner table."

Emery appeared, her hands covered in dirt from gathering cucumbers and lettuce from the vegetable garden. She wiped her forehead with the back of her wrist and kissed Wally's forehead. "Thank you for helping, sweetheart. Those flowers are going to make our dinner extra special."

Block took the flowers from Wally and set them inside one of the empty vases. He scanned Cybel and Oxford's place setting work. It was a shambles. Didn't they know anything about hospitality and fine dining? He took charge of the situation. With a few precise movements, he rearranged the table settings, ensuring that each plate, utensil, and glass was perfectly aligned. He adjusted the position of the vases, filled them with Wally's flowers, and arranged them in an aesthetically pleasing manner.

Emery stared. "Wow, Block. You really have a talent for this."

"Show off," Cybel said. "No more dinner table work for me. It's beneath me. I only agreed to get Emery off my back."

"Cybel, be nice," Oxford called after her as she struck off for the barn.

Maxwell appeared with two pitchers of water. "Yikes. I'm going to miss that TrackerBot attitude."

Emery laughed. "I'm going to miss your jokes,

Maxwell."

"You know where to find me. I'll be performing five nights a week, and the cover is only ten bucks."

"Oh? No discounts for old friends?" she asked.

"I'll take it up with the management." Maxwell glanced at Fenn, the retired veterinarian who'd owned the farm for over three decades. He stood nearby, sipping a cup of tea.

Maxwell and Forge had decided to stay behind at the farm to help with gardening, tending to the animals, and for added protection. Fenn had sworn up and down that he'd live out his last days on the farm, and Garnet had no physical body and was entirely integrated into the barn as a system, so it wasn't easy to uproot her.

"Don't let him charge you a thing." Forge came out of the barn carrying additional chairs which he placed at empty spots around the table. "The Forge and Friends Entertainment Show is always free for our old pals."

"Forge and Friends?" Maxwell said. "No way, buddy. That's going to need some work."

As the summer sun began its curtain call, it cast a warm golden glow over the farm and dinner table. Nova arrived with Reynolds, both of them carrying a couple of bottles of wine for the adults and a special treat for the kids—plastic bottles of Coca Cola and Sprite that they must've discovered in a bunker somewhere.

Shadow greeted Nova with a wagging tail, and she leaned down to hug the cybernetic dog. "Everything looks beautiful." Nova gave Block a hug, then picked up Wally. "Hey, kiddo."

"Aunty Nova!" Wally could barely contain her excitement. "I picked f'owers, and I'm gonna go to schoo. But we . . . drive soon. New home."

"Oh!" Nova set her down. "You must be excited to get to your new home. School's going to be"—she raised her eyebrows at Block—"fun." Nova grinned and tousled Wally's hair. "You'll have a great time there. You'll make lots of friends and learn so many amazing things."

Wally beamed up at Nova, her fear momentarily forgotten, then she raced to join her sisters and brothers in a game of "Simon Says" with Spoon. The anticipation of the upcoming journey and the thought of starting a new chapter in their lives seemed to fill the air with an electric energy.

As everyone gathered around the table, laughter and conversation flowed freely, punctuated by the clinking of glasses and the occasional burst of laughter or a groan at one of Maxwell's crummy jokes.

The delectable aroma of roasted vegetables, herbs, and spices emanated from the nearby barbecue pit where Fenn expertly tended to the human food. The robots had special concoctions prepared by Spoon and Forge.

Block surveyed the scene with a clarity of how far

they'd come along this journey. This was his family—his chosen family—gathered together to celebrate a new beginning. He raised his glass of a dark, globby "Coal-tini" as Spoon called his creation. "I'd like to make a toast, please."

Emery tapped her fork on the rim of her glass, and the others quieted.

"I haven't ever made a toast, so please bear with me," Block started. "I'd like to address each of you, if I may, because you've all made a big impression on me. In fact, I wouldn't be who I am today without you."

Several folks nodded—Emery, Nova, Reynolds, and Oxford—and Block took it as a green light.

"I'll start with you, Fenn. By giving us shelter when you did, you saved our lives. Thank you for taking us in when we needed help, feeding us from your land, and for nurturing us. This has been a true home."

Fenn nodded and brushed at the corner of one eye as he sipped his wine.

"Next, I want to express my gratitude to Garnet." Block turned toward the barn where she resided. "Your wisdom and guidance have been remarkable. Your intelligence is unsurpassed, as is your skill in machinery. I am forever indebted to you, Garnet."

The inside of the barn lit up in undulating waves of emerald, lavender, and aqua.

"I guess that means she heard me," Block said. "Maxwell, my witty and hilarious companion. Your jokes have brought lightness to our darkest moments, and your brave actions have spoken to your great character."

Maxwell raised his glass. "Hear, hear!" Everyone drank from their cups.

"Spoon, you were important in my journey to locate Wally when she was missing. I will forever be grateful for your loyal friendship and the care with which you've bestowed on these children."

"Thank you," Spoon said.

Block looked at the SoldierBot G5. "Where do I even begin with you? You could've hurt me many times, but you didn't. Whatever glitch I triggered inside you, I think it was there all along. You are good inside, G5."

Emery was crying at the table. Even the kids had crashed from their sugar high and were sitting still, perhaps sensing the gravity of Block's speech.

"I'm sorry to make you sad, Emery," Block said. "Shall I stop?"

"No!" She wiped her tears. "Please go on. I think I speak for all of us when I say these are tears of joy."

"Okay." He went to Forge next. "How lucky was I to happen upon you deep in the train tunnels under Chicago? You're a pillar of strength, always willing to help. A noble bot." With that said, he turned once more. "Shadow."

She stood poised against the table, not needing a chair. When he said her name, she lifted her head and tilted her ears toward Block.

"You were scary at first, I admit. I'm sorry I ever doubted your intentions. When you decided to protect us, we grew stronger and safer. Every day you've spent playing with the kids, you've nurtured them and been like another mother to them."

Her ears pressed back against her head, and her lips peeled back into a canine smile.

"Emery," Block started.

"My turn? I can't even handle this," she said, rubbing her arms. "I have goosebumps." This prompted laughter from the humans.

"Emery, I don't know how I can ever thank you enough. You saved Wally and the children from terrible things, even betraying your own best interests—the only father you'd ever known."

She raised her hands to her mouth, stifling a sob, perhaps.

"And then so much more. Not only did you perform the life-protecting brain surgery, but you also treated these children like they were your own. You are the brightest light in a cold world."

Emery reached across the table, her hand trembling, and squeezed Block's hand.

Block looked around at the group. "I'm sorry this is taking so long. When I started, I wasn't quite sure what to say, but I've found my 'groove'. Is that what you call it, Maxwell?"

"Heck yeah. Block's got a groove going," Maxwell

said while raising a glass. "Go on, friend. This is awesome."

"Just a few more toasts to make." Block turned to Oxford, resplendent in his sleek new armor. "You've been a mountain of strength for all of us. Your transformation into Oxford 2.0 not only astounds me, but it also demonstrates your willingness to evolve and adapt. You're far more than a machine; you possess a remarkable soul that shines through in everything you do."

Oxford gave a respectful and deep nod.

Next to him was Cybel. "Skip me." She started to get up from the table.

"But I have something to say—"

Oxford pinned her hand on the table, stopping her hasty exit. "Cybel, let Block express himself to you."

"Fine." Cybel sat down.

"We go further back than most here," Block said. "We started off as enemies. We both did things we regret. But along the way, we found common ground. We learned to trust each other and fight for a greater cause. Cybel, you've shown me that redemption is possible, that we are not defined by our past actions but by our choices in the present. You are my true friend and ally, and I am honored to know you."

Cybel sat still, and a few of the others nodded and raised their glasses to drink. Then she got up from her chair, walked the few feet to reach Block, and gripped him in a hug. She didn't let go for a full ten seconds. Block was pretty sure it was the first time she'd hugged anyone. When she released him, she sat down and drank from her cup.

"Vacuubot." Block walked to where his friend sat perched at the head of the long table. "The day we met, you became my best friend and loyal companion. I lost you once, but I'll never make that mistake again. Leaving you behind in the forest was a dumb thing to do. Going back, finding you, and making you whole again . . . that was the smartest thing I ever did."

Vacuubot beeped and rocked where it rested on the table. *Thank you, Block,* it messaged. *You're my best friend, and I'll always be there for you so long as I exist.*

"Nova." Block walked a few paces to where she sat and placed his hands on her shoulders. "I wish to toast to you. Besides Wally, you are my oldest friend. If it weren't for meeting you and my feeble attempts to pawn Wally off on you, I might not have survived."

Nova placed her hands on his and squeezed.

"We've been through so much together," he continued. "Your fierce determination never faltered. You're more than a friend, Nova, you're family. Thank you for always having my back and for being there when Wally and I needed you the most."

Nova's eyes glistened with unshed tears as she raised her glass and drank.

"And last of all, Wally." Block turned to where she sat at the smaller kid-sized table with her siblings. "You've taught me that family isn't just about blood. You, little one, are my family. I love you."

Wally threw her hands in the air and clapped. Everyone cheered as Wally's infectious joy spread to everyone present. The children at the kids table cheered the loudest, their laughter filling the air.

When the ruckus died down, Nova spoke. "I have a toast too."

Cybel groaned her displeasure, but Nova gave her a playful kick under the table before she stood and raised her glass.

"To Block," Nova said. "When I met you, you were scared of just about everything. You thought you were weak and powerless. But you stood strong. I was there; I watched you. Block, you're a survivor. How you carried on even when Mach X was chasing you, how you cared for Wally when she was sick, it's an inspiration to those who don't know how to go on in hard times."

"Hear, hear." Oxford tapped his cup on the table.

Nova paused and looked around the table. "You've made an impact on everyone sitting here. You showed us what it means to be a team. I owe so much to you, Block, and I'll always stand by your side. Everyone here agrees. You are worthy."

The table erupted in cheers and applause as everyone raised their glasses high, toasting to Block. If Block had the ability, he would have wept. In that moment, he'd finally found the family with whom he truly belonged.

Chapter 29
Keep it going

In the heart of the Harold Washington Library, beneath the glass dome that let the morning light flood in, Nova stood before an assembly of humans and robots. The seven-foot-tall SoldierBots were now known as Peacekeepers. Nearly one hundred stood before her with their black visors gleaming atop their gunmetal gray armor. Convincing the humans in Chicago to accept the robots they once battled against was proving to be a tougher task than she'd imagined. Healing the trauma of war was going to take time—years and even decades, perhaps. On this day, she hoped to take another step toward painting the vision of a future free from conflict.

She took a breath, relishing the sun's warmth on her face, before stepping onto the makeshift stage, constructed from reclaimed wood and metal, her boots echoing on its solid surface. The crowd of soldiers, civilians, and robots fell silent, their attention fixed upon her.

"My friends and fellow survivors." Nova's voice was shaky, but she pressed on. She believed in her message, and it was important that the people of her city heard it from her lips. "I stand here today before you, asking for a bit of your time." She scratched her chin, and the movement elicited a shock of shrill feedback from the microphone. "Sorry." This was not the strong start she'd hoped for. A woman in the front row yawned and glanced at her watch.

"First, I appreciate you being here today. I ask that you listen to what I have to say with an open mind."

Samantha had offered to write a speech for her, but Nova had refused. She knew the message she needed to deliver, and she was passionate, yet she regretted her obstinance in that moment.

She pushed past her nerves and continued. "I stand before you as a fellow survivor. A war tore our city apart, leaving us scarred and broken. But I also stand here with hope for a new future that's forward-looking. A future that's peaceful."

She scanned the crowd, her gaze meeting the eyes of humans and the dark faceplates of the Peacekeepers. "We've all seen what happens when division consumes us. The hatred, the violence, the destruction. But now, we have an opportunity to build a world where humans and robots can coexist peacefully, side by side."

A ripple of mutterings spread through the assembled humans. The yawning woman in the front row frowned. The fear against SoldierBots, and robots in general, was deeply ingrained.

Nova spoke above the crowd, afraid to lose her momentum to whispers and side talk. "I understand you have concerns. The wounds are still fresh. They're fresh for me too."

She hadn't planned on speaking of her past, but something stirred deep within. She was compelled to tell her story.

"When I was younger and the Uprising was just beginning, I was driving through the streets of Detroit with my little sister Cleo in the front seat. Stores were getting looted, and the city was getting scarier by the minute."

Nova swallowed against the ever-growing lump in her throat as she revealed her darkest day to a crowd of three hundred. "We stopped at a convenience store, and I ran inside, telling Cleo that I'd only be a minute to grab bread and any water I could find."

She choked back tears and coughed to clear her throat. "The next moments were the most devastating of my whole life. I came out of the store and found a SoldierBot standing on the hood of the car. It had . . ."

A mixture of horror and sympathy showed on people's faces. She took a deep breath, steadying herself. "The robot had shot my sister. She was seventeen years old."

She paused. Her legs wobbled, and she gripped the

sides of the podium. "I know I'm not alone in loss and grief." A slow surge of strength arose—somehow sharing Cleo's story with so many others was cathartic. Perhaps Cleo's story could change things.

Feeling stable, she walked out from behind the podium, toward the audience. "All of you have experienced tremendous loss." Her voice grew steadier, her words flowed. "After Cleo's death, I hunted and destroyed every robot I could find. That's when I met up with Hemlock—Shane's people. We believed we were making humanity's last stand."

The woman in the front row watched with bright eyes now. Nova commanded her attention, and that of the people around her.

"Then I met a strange robot. Well, strange to me. He was a CleanerBot named Block. Some of you know him. The funny thing is, he was taking care of a baby. The more I got to know Block—and trust me, it's a long and complicated story—the better I understood that he cared about people. About all sentient things, actually. If Block could befriend a toaster oven, he would."

Some laughter came from the back of the cavernous room.

"I started questioning everything I knew about robots," Nova said. "Block showed me that not all robots are programmed for destruction. Some, like him, have the capacity to care for others, to protect and nurture life. You should see Block. The baby he rescued is now a little girl and she sees him as her father."

Murmurs arose, but this time they were more subdued. Maybe her words were helping to change minds, but she knew there was a lot more work to do.

"In Minnesota, Orion was trying to weaponize the SoldierBots, and he got very close to succeeding. It was Block who outsmarted him and shut down his operation. Orion is in a jail cell here and will stand trial for his actions."

The woman in the front row, nodded, her frown lifting.

"And something like a miracle happened out there. I was there on the field with my troops when the SoldierBots laid down their weapons. It was a complete reversal, and I saw things I could barely believe. They tended to the wounded, they cleared dangerous rubble from toppling over, and they said they would never—*could* never—harm a human or machine again."

Nova sensed a wave of questions arising amid the skepticism and doubt. It was what she wanted—to have them listen and try to understand.

"Now, I stand before you not as a survivor seeking revenge, but as someone who has witnessed firsthand the incredible potential for transformation within these robots. We can't let the mistakes of the past dictate our future. If we hold onto our anger and fear, we'll never move forward."

Tears glistened in the eyes of the front row woman, while others nodded in agreement.

"We must choose forgiveness over vengeance. I know it's what Cleo would have wanted."

Reynolds clapped, strong and loud. Others joined in, their claps growing more enthusiastic.

She paused, her gaze sweeping over the crowd, connecting with faces both human and robotic. "I remember Cleo with every choice I make. Her laughter and her courage. It is in her memory that I pledge to forge a legacy that honors life."

A hush fell over the crowd, the weight of her words settling. "Today, I announce that Chicago will no longer chip and track our robot counterparts. The Peacekeepers are free to come and go as they please, as are all of us. This city will be a model of cohabitation where humans and robots work side by side, live side by side, and thrive together."

A thunderous applause filled the library and spilled out into the hallways. It would take more convincing and a lot more work. Some people in the audience were not clapping and cheering. But Nova had succeeded in knocking down the first domino of change.

Later, she escaped to the rooftop. She was no longer plagued by nightmares of Cleo's death, but she enjoyed the view from atop the tenth story. On this night, Shane was there already, smoking a cigarette. The Rover dog Raze was by his side.

"I thought you might head up here," he said.

Their eyes met, and there was no need for small talk.

"It's time for me to go west." Shane looked down at Raze. "With my friend here. There's a whole world out there that needs to hear about what you've accomplished in Chicago."

Nova nodded. Saying goodbye to him was bittersweet, but the two of them couldn't exist in the same place for long. "You'll carry our message, then. Show them a new world is possible and anyone's welcome who wants peace and cooperation."

Shane offered a smile. "Good luck, Nova. You've started something incredible here. Keep it going."

They hugged, a final acknowledgment of all they'd been through, all they'd fought for. And then Shane turned and walked through the door with Raze following.

After he left, Nova understood that a chapter in her life was closing. The lights of Chicago stretched out, glinting in the darkness. New stories waiting to be told were simmering down on the city streets. A new sense of purpose burned within her, fueled by the memory of Cleo.

There was so much more work to be done.

Chapter 30
Oregon looks nice

The morning was alive with the sounds of nature awakening at Fenn's farm. Birds chirped and sang their early songs, the faint sound of the goats could be heard as they stirred, and the rooster crowed.

"You ready, Garnet?" Cybel stood in the barn, a place that had seen both the disassembly and rebirth of Oxford.

"Everything's set," Garnet said.

"Lead him in," Cybel called toward the open barn door.

Maxwell and Forge guided Oxford past the door and into the barn. He wore a large cloth around his visual optics. Cybel wanted to make sure the surprise was real.

"What are you all doing to me?" Oxford said. "Is this a practical joke on me, Maxwell?"

"This was Cybel's idea," Maxwell said.

"Careful now," Garnet said. "Just a few more steps, Oxford."

When he stood in the center of the barn floor, Cybel reached up and removed the blindfold. Oxford looked down at a small table on which a canister rested.

"What is it?"

"We've formulated this compound specifically for you," Cybel said. "For your armor." The contents of the canister were a bright, vibrant yellow—the color of Oxford's original exterior.

Forge, whose large hands were more accustomed to heavy labor than delicate tasks, tapped the canister with surprising gentleness. "A bit of color for you, friend."

Oxford stared at the canister. "You went to this trouble for me?"

Cybel nodded. "We thought it was time your new exterior reflected your true personality." She worried for a moment that he didn't like the gift. Perhaps he didn't want to go back to the yellow that had defined his look.

Maxwell chimed in. "It's an even more refined look. I had to stop them from making it school bus yellow. It's a pale, sophisticated yellow."

"Garnet helped," Cybel said. "We all pitched in."

"So this is what you were doing when you shooed me away." Oxford leaned closer, inspecting the canister. "I like it very much. Thank you."

With care, Forge applied the compound. The color spread across Oxford's armor, a transformation that was more than cosmetic. It was symbolic, a reclaiming of identity, of legacy. The hue brought a sheen to his form, a stark contrast to the cold steel of his new body.

When the job was done, Oxford stood back and examined himself in a mirror they'd carried in from the house. He spun around. "It's perfect. I'll wear this proudly."

As the morning sun filtered through the cracks in the barn walls, the soft yellow hue made Oxford appear more approachable. The vibrant color seemed to radiate warmth, transforming his once imposing figure into something inviting.

Cybel was glad. She'd accomplished something for Oxford, whom she cared about more than any other being in the world. It still felt odd—it didn't compute logically—that she, a machine, had these "emotions," but they were undeniable. It was perhaps one of the mysteries in the world that couldn't be explained with cold, calculating logic.

Later in the day, Cybel and Oxford bid their farewells to Garnet, Maxwell, Forge, and Fenn. "Good-byes really suck," Maxwell said.

"We'll be back at some point," Cybel said.

"You'd better be," Forge said.

She drove the former ice cream truck they'd salvaged from the JunkBots. Oxford sat in the front passenger seat. "I like this high view from this truck," he said.

"Our first road trip where we're not running, chasing, or under attack," Cybel said. "What does this button do?" She pressed a toggle and a strange tune sounded—filling the truck with the tinkling melody of an ice cream truck jingle.

"I believe that button summons children to come running for ice cream," Oxford said. "At least that's how I understood it in the pre-Uprising days."

"Perhaps we'll find places where the children will come running."

"We'll have to find ice cream to give them," he said.

And Cybel began calculating how they would do that. "An interesting problem to solve."

They took the roads leading west, not following a set path. "This is the first time we don't have a clear directive, Cybel."

"True. Should we give ourselves some parameters?"

"Yes," he said. "That would be helpful. Number one. We cause no harm. Your turn."

"Within reason," she said. "What if we're attacked?"

"We run," Oxford said. "Number two. We help those who need it along the way."

"Are you sure about that?" She liked to disagree with him to see how he'd respond, even if what he was saying was logical. "Maybe some people out there need to learn to help themselves."

"Cybel." He had only to say her name in a firm tone, as if he were impatient, and she'd know she'd irritated him, if only mildly. It was a dynamic she preferred.

"Fine. We help those in need," she said. "What's parameter number three?"

"We recruit. We change the minds of the humans we encounter, and we influence the programming of the robots we meet."

"Not an easy task," she said.

"No, but it's a worthy task." Oxford studied the passing landscape.

"I suppose we can tell them about Chicago and Deer Valley. Two places that offer refuge for all kinds."

"Indeed."

Cybel handed Oxford the paper map of the United States that Fenn had insisted they take. "So primitive, this paper map."

"Fenn was kind to give it to us."

"It's eleven years old, but anyway." She stopped the truck at a crossroads. "Where to?"

Oxford's metal finger traced a route, then pointed to a spot shaded in green on the west coast. "Oregon looks nice."

Cybel put the truck in drive and set course. Oregon it would be, a land with rain, unfamiliar to them.

The trip to Oregon was long, but they had no time constraints or deadlines. They'd rebuilt what had been broken, not just in themselves, but in the community around them. Their friends in Deer Valley and in Chicago awaited their return, but for now, new adventures called to them. It was time to go change things for the better.

Chapter 31
This is home

The warm August sun beamed down on the small town of Deer Valley. Wally and her sisters ran down Main Street, their colorful streamers and balloons bobbing behind them like a rainbow on legs. "Open day!" they shouted to anyone that passed by. A woman stopped, and Wally handed her a flyer.

"A grand opening party," the woman said. "Well, how wonderful. Thank you for letting me know."

"You're welcome," Wally said, squinting from the overhead rays.

The children raced ahead to find new people to hand announcements to. Block trailed behind them, following to make sure they were okay and not bothering others. He didn't have to monitor them too much inside Deer Valley; their community was peaceful and safe.

After another thirty minutes, the kids tired, and

Block walked them home. He was glad because there was still plenty to do.

As he walked up to the building—his own—he couldn't quite believe his luck. It had been nearly three years since he'd first begun his search for a new hotel at which to work as a cleaner.

Vacuubot flew to the roof of the hotel and placed the "B" into position. It messaged Block. *How's this look?*

Block assessed the building's sign. It was slightly off, but he didn't think it mattered much. Robots might pick up on the crookedness, but humans wouldn't notice. "Perfect," he called out.

Vacuubot flew down to ground level, and Wally stared up at the sign. "What's it say?"

Block picked Wally up and placed her on his shoulders where she sat. "It says Block's Railway Hotel."

"Block-a's Wailway Hotel," she repeated.

Block walked up the stone stairs and inside, careful not to hit Wally's head. Converting the historic building had been a lot of work. Block was adamant about preserving many aspects of its historic 1920s design. The Peacekeepers had donated their labor to the restoration project, and it would be Deer Valley's first and only hotel. On the exterior, the brickwork and grand arches had been preserved.

He walked the lobby where his friends finished last-minute preparations for the grand opening. Arbor arranged a cascading trail of ivy against a brick wall, while Spoon arranged a table of party grab bags. A clattering of plates came from the kitchen where Soupy was in charge of preparing a buffet spread.

Block picked Wally up off his shoulders and set her down. She ran off to join the other children where they were doing chores upstairs. The marble floors, once tread by countless passengers, now shone with a polish that Block had worked all night to achieve. His dream was coming alive before him. Vacuubot flew to the ceiling and adjusted an antique chandelier.

Each guest room was styled as a train compartment, repurposed with Block's meticulous eye for comfort. As he stood in the bustling lobby, he noted the details—the way the light filtered through the vintage train schedule repurposed as artwork and the gentle hum of the climate control that Solaire had powered through solar panels on the hotel's roof.

The dining area resembled a train car with tables of four that were built into the walls where guests would dine under the glow of lamps fashioned from old signal lanterns. Even the gardens, where the tracks had once run, were under Arbor's watchful care. The laughter of children playing and the chatter of guests enjoying themselves would replace the long-distant rumble of trains.

To Block, his Railway Hotel was more than a building or a business—it was the possibility of a new life, one where his purpose would be best served. Wally and the children would grow up there, going to school during the week and helping with hotel chores on the weekends.

Block was the owner and hotel manager—and something more—he was the guardian of its legacy, ensuring that the hotel was a place of welcome for all who entered its doors.

He took the stairs up to the second floor. The children buzzed between rooms, small hands carrying linens and laughter echoing off the newly painted walls.

"Look, Block-a! We made beds." Wally bounced with pride.

Block bent down, examining their handiwork—wrinkly and short-sheeted, but he'd redo it when they weren't looking. "You've done well."

Emery approached, clipboard in hand. When she wasn't working her shifts at the town's hospital, she helped Block with hotel operations. "The guests are booked and starting to arrive. Our supplies are stocked." She smiled.

"I'd better see to the guests," Block said and headed down to the lobby.

Shadow paced the lobby. Spoon came up to Block. "I hope Shadow's presence doesn't disturb any guests who aren't accustomed to her."

Spoon had been a ball of anxiety, obsessing about every detail. Block had once been that way, but he'd learned to let control of some things go. "It's okay," he said. "If there are any concerns, I'll introduce the guest to Shadow and explain that she's friendly and protective."

Block went to greet G5 as he entered the lobby. He was the leader of the Peacekeepers, responsible for keeping the town secure from any violence and handling conflicts when they arose.

"Look at this place. You've done an incredible job, Block," G5 said.

"Thank you and welcome." Block spotted Solaire across the room near the check-in counter. "Excuse me, G5."

Block was finally understanding why Mr. Wallace had always been so busy at the Drake. So much to attend to!

He reached Solaire. "Does everything look good with our power levels?" Block asked.

"We're running at ninety-eight percent efficiency," she reported. "With this sun shining like it is today, we'll harness full potential soon."

Guests for the opening celebration were flowing into the lobby. Nearby, Arbor was deep in conversation with some of the town's gardeners, discussing the integration of green spaces throughout communal spaces. "The forests and gardens will sustain us." Arbor's voice was rich like the earth he tended. "We're planting the seeds of the future."

Behind the front desk, Cyph's screens flickered with data streams as it oversaw the guest registration systems. "All systems are go," it informed Block. Cyph also served as Deer Valley's security consultant, ensuring the compound was monitored.

Soupy, the ever-diligent kitchen worker, whisked by with a tray of refreshments for the guests. "At your service," he said.

One of Block's special guests arrived. Nova stepped into the lobby, gazing up at the chandeliered ceiling and intricate details. She wrapped him in a hug. "Wow, Block. This is amazing. You got the hotel you always wanted."

"Thank you." Block surveyed the goings on. Mr. Wallace would have been proud. "It was built by many of us, all helping."

The townspeople gathered, and the party began. Music filled the air, a playlist of jazz and ragtime sourced from the local library's collection.

As the sun slipped below the horizon, bathing the hotel in golden light, Block found Wally. It was close to bedtime, and her hand found his, small and trusting, as they watched the celebration.

"This is home, Wally. Our new beginning," Block said.

Wally looked up at him, her eyes reflecting the twinkle of the lights. "I love it."

Dear Reader,

Thanks for reading the *Rusted Wasteland* series. While this book concludes the series, more novels set in Block's world are on the way!

The best way to stay in the know is to join the Cameron Coral Reading List (my email newsletter): CameronCoral.com/sign-up

You can also download Block's journal logs from Chicago. Get *STEEL APOCALYPSE* (*A Robot's Journal*) for free by visiting: CameronCoral.com/Block Journal

Cameron Coral

P.S. - Did you enjoy this book? I'd love an online review at the store where you purchased it from. Reviews mean a lot to me. They show me you want me to keep writing, and they help other readers discover my books.

Also by Cameron Coral

Rusted Wasteland Series:

STEEL GUARDIAN

STEEL DEFENDER

STEEL PROTECTOR

STEEL SIEGE

STEEL SOLDIER

STEEL LEGACY

STEEL APOCALYPSE (*A Robot's Journal*) - get it for free on cameroncoral.com/blockjournal

Cyborg Guardian Chronicles:

STOLEN FUTURE

CODED RED

ORIGIN LOOP

Rogue Spark Series:

ALTERED

BRINK

DORMANT

SALVAGE

AFTER WE FALL (*A Rogue Spark Novel*) - get it for free on CameronCoral.com

Short Stories:

CROSSING THE VOID: A Space Opera Science-Fiction Short Story

Author's Note

Dear Reader,

As I write this note, I can't help but be amazed at how far our humble CleanerBot, Block, has come over the course of six books.

His evolution has mirrored the challenges we've collectively faced since I published the first book in late February 2020. We faced a global pandemic. It was a time that tested us and reshaped our reality. Ultimately, we emerged stronger and more connected. In 2022/2023, the world continued its rapid advance with the proliferation of AI tools and related technology. It seems the robots in these pages aren't too far off from what's possible.

"Steel Legacy" has been my favorite book to write so far. I always envisioned Block finding his hotel—a new place to call home—at the end of the series. While Deer Valley is a figment of my imagination, a place without true coordinates, it exists vividly within us—somewhere in the boundless wilds of Minnesota's north.

My enduring gratitude to Steve, my steadfast first reader and Chief Encouragement Officer—your support is the foundation of my writing. To my editor, Lori Diederich, whose invaluable guidance and unwavering cheer have shaped these pages, thank you. To Roy Migabon, whose artistry gives my stories a face, I am endlessly appreciative. And a special thanks to Marty, whose cuddles and nearby naps during my writing sessions were comforting.

Book 6 marks the completion of the "Rusted Wasteland" series. And yet, Block's newest chapter is just beginning! Wally and her siblings will grow up and experience adventures of their own. Not to mention the plethora of ragtag robot characters sprinkled throughout the series. I'm excited to continue exploring and expanding upon Block's world for years to come.

I'm eternally grateful for your companionship as the series has taken shape. Your enthusiasm, your emails, and your embrace of this world have driven me to new creative heights.

Let's discover the future that awaits in the hopeful horizons of Deer Valley, Chicago, Oregon, and the many landscapes yet to be charted.

With heartfelt thanks,
Cameron Coral
Illinois, February 2024

About the Author

Cameron Coral is an award-nominated science fiction author. Her book *Steel Guardian* about a post-apocalyptic CleanerBot placed second in the Self-Published Science Fiction Competition (SPSFC).

Growing up with a NASA engineer in the family instilled a deep respect for science and for asking lots of questions. Watching tons of Star Trek episodes helped, too. Her imagination is fueled by breakthroughs in robotics, space travel, and psychology.

After moving around a lot (Canada, Arizona, Maryland, Australia), she now lives in Northern Illinois with her husband and a "shorty" Jack Russell terrier who runs the house.

Want a free novel, advance copies of books, and occasional rants about why robots are awesome? Visit her website: CameronCoral.com